LOVE IS BLUE

When the phone rings she knows it is Piero—she has been waiting for his call on Christmas Day. The hospital room is filled with his flowers, her heart is filled with love. It has been so long since they touched or kissed; his is the only face she can picture in her mind.

She can hear Greg say to him, "Yes, she is doing well. Do you want to talk to her?"

"No," she says. "No. I won't talk to him."

"Come on, Bettina, why not?"

My God, why not?

If I touch the phone I will be touching him. I am ugly now, and he is so beautiful. If I enter his world he will lose that beauty; I will alter his reality—his peace will become pain. I love him too much to take happiness away from him.

Bettina cries softly as she hears Greg say goodbye. She needs and wants Piero so much. But she is all alone—and always will be. All she has now is her memories . . .

SOMETHING FOR EVERYONE—
BEST SELLERS FROM ZEBRA!

FRIENDS (645, $2.25)
by Elieba Levine
Edith and Sarah had been friends for thirty years, sharing all their secrets and fantasies. No one ever thought that a bond as close as theirs could be broken . . . but now underneath the friendship and love is jealousy, anger, and hate.

EPIDEMIC! (644, $2.50)
by Larry R. Leichter, M.D.
From coast to coast, beach to beach, the killer virus spread. Diagnosed as a strain of meningitis, it did not respond to treatment—and no one could stop it from becoming the world's most terrifying epidemic!

ALL THE WAY (571, $2.25)
by Felice Buckvar
After over twenty years of devotion to another man, Phyllis finds herself helplessly in love, once again, with that same tall, handsome high school sweetheart who had loved her . . . ALL THE WAY.

RHINELANDER PAVILLION (572, $2.50)
by Barbara Harrison
Rhinelander Pavillion was a big city hospital pulsating with the constant struggles of life and death. Its dedicated staff of overworked professionals were caught up in the unsteady charts of their own passions and desires—yet they all needed medicine to survive.

Available wherever paperbacks are sold, or order direct from the Publisher. Send cover price plus 50¢ per copy for mailing and handling to Zebra Books, 21 East 40th Street, New York, N.Y. 10016. DO NOT SEND CASH!

The Vow

By Maria B. Fogelin

ZEBRA BOOKS
KENSINGTON PUBLISHING CORP.

ZEBRA BOOKS

are published by

KENSINGTON PUBLISHING CORP.
21 East 40th Street
New York, N.Y. 10016

Copyright © 1980 by Maria B. Fogelin

All rights reserved. No part of this book may be reproduced in any form or by any means without the prior written consent of the Publisher, excepting brief quotes used in reveiws.

Printed in the United States of America

For my thinking daughters
Julia Adrian and Claudia Maria

and for my tolerant son
Carl Christian

She can hear the murmur of voices, a calm efficient mumbling, and she feels her pain, her incredible pain. She is screaming, but there is no sound in her ears, she is screaming down a corridor of hell.

She waited at the exit from the shopping center, barely seeing the cars coming from the other direction through the slashing rain. The old VW had been sitting in the driveway for two weeks and the motor was stuttering, shaking her slightly on the worn seat. *If I don't move, I'll stall,* she was thinking. *Wouldn't that be my luck, to have the car break down so that I have to call Greg to come and rescue me. That ought to do something for the surprise element of his birthday party.* Beside her on the seat of the VW was a small brown bag with a slip of white paper stapled to it

```
       NORTON'S

       .39 pty gds
       .02 tx
       .41 ttl

       thank you
```

containing blue birthday candles for her brother Greg's cake. It was the reason she was out now in this storm. For thirty-nine cents of wax and wick she was about to risk apocalypse and lose.

The voices around her are fluctuating like a badly tuned radio
   they are cutting away her clothing, she

feels the coolness of the scissors sliding across her belly releasing her
she is naked
Oh God oh God what's happening to me
what's happened

She was six years old and she was going into the operating room of Mercy Hospital to have her tonsils taken out. She was scared because they wouldn't let her mother come with her. "I'll be right here when you get out, *cara*," her mother called after her. "Be a good girl."

Now they were putting the anesthetic into her arm. She had her eyes closed, but she could feel the needle go in. Almost at once the voices began to *wahh-wahh*.

"Count backwards for me, sweetheart," the doctor said cheerfully, and he prompted her, "Ten . . ."

* * *

"Nine," she whispered, obeying. "Eight..." She didn't hear him say, "Good girl."

Then her mother was saying, "It's all over, *cara*. That wasn't so bad, was it? Look, here's the Barbie doll I promised you." And Bettina had wanted that Barbie doll more than anything she'd ever known, more than catechism promises of paradise, but the pain in her throat was so dreadfully dreadful, she had not known it was possible for there to be so much pain, and she had difficulty making her fingers close around the stiff doll her mother put in her hand.

She can feel a chill on her skin, her bare skin is wet. "Here, wipe with this," a woman's voice says sharply, and there is the sensation of cloth touching her quickly, gently, on her breast, but the wetness remains.

It was raining hard. She lay in the wreckage of her car, hearing the *sirens and men's shouts of Oh God hurry oh God why the fucking oh God she's going hurry it up will you will you will you*

she felt the rain, felt the rain falling through her, she was inundated with moisture, more than storms, more than oceans, and she caught the smell of her own blood

they were cutting away the metal, she could hear the sound, she could feel the heat, and she fainted and returned and fainted again, it was her body's gift to her, the brief moments of unconsciousness in the wild paroxysm of pain and she did not yet realize the darkness.

They are cutting her hair. In that overwhelming red push of pain, she can feel the small movement in her scalp as they pick up strands of her hair, her hair that she hasn't cut since the sixth grade, her hair that is her identity. She can hear the *scrunch scrunch* of the blades of the scissors coming together behind her ear cutting her hair, and she screams at them, *Don't cut it* but her lips have not moved, and she knows she made no sound. She concentrates, fighting strangers and this peculiar state of her body, she draws herself up tight into her incredible head, trying to remember how to operate her mouth

and the scissors are going around the back of her head, she can feel hands turning her to get at her hair, she hears the light swish of it shoved off the table, she must hurry and tell these people or it will be too late

but no one responds to her screech of agony, and she tries it again, snorting blood, she jerks it in anguish through her nose, "Please . . ."

"Wait a minute," somebody says. "Didn't she just say something?"

"That's impossible."

"I don't care if it's impossible, I think she said something."

"Please . . ." she breathes again. It is a sound.

For an instant, everything around her stops. "Dammit, she *did* say something. Didn't you hear her?"

"What is it, honey?" a woman's voice asks gently. "What are you trying to say?"

"Don't . . ."

"Don't what? What's her name, does any-

body know?"
"Bettina. I think her name's Bettina."
"Don't what, Bettina?"

There was twilight falling on her face, weak twilight painted on her skin with freezing wind. The students running up the steps toward Low Library were wearing knitted caps and breathing dragons' breath. She was so cold that she was stumbling, but only numbly aware of it, she was looking about her with wondering eyes at the familiar buildings sketched in shadows, suddenly they were unbearably beautiful, being alive now, this instant, walking the everyday cement of her campus with Piero's arm around her was unbearably beautiful.

She grabbed his waist with both of her arms, murmuring almost incoherently, "This can't last, you know that, don't you? This isn't real life . . ."

They had stopped halfway up the

steps to look at each other. He was smiling at her. "Sh," he said. "Sh." Then he gently lifted a strand of her hair and looped it around the back of his neck, pulling it slowly in an exquisitely sensuous movement so that her face was drawn to his, their mouths approached inexorably, they were tied together with her long long hair.

"Don't . . . cut . . . my hair . . ."
"Sorry about that, honey, but you've got a hole as big as Grand Central Station in your head."
"But . . . I'm getting married . . ."
and yet, all of her fantastic effort of concentration, of pulling together the bits of her soul that are escaping her in all directions through a dozen fissures in her body, doesn't stop them, they can't care about her wanting to keep her hair, her wanting to walk to Piero Ferrari with white roses entwined in her hip-length black hair, she can feel them going on with cutting, they move her unresisting head, cutting and cutting

they tell her distractedly, "We'll worry about the wedding later, kiddo," for she is a body with a hole as big as Grand Central Station in its head, she's been unlucky and gotten herself into this mess and it's up to them to get her out of it

she feels the coolness of the liquid soap being smoothed into her scalp, she smells its ugly surgical scent and knows the jerking glide of the razor baring her skull, she isn't a young woman any longer, she is a smooth and repulsive embryo

and she hates her nakedness and the impersonal hands that touch her and the sound her hair makes falling on the floor, her stomach cannot contain the hatred, she is retching, ashamed of this additional ugliness but her stomach heaves

it has been so long since she has eaten that all she has in her stomach is bitter juices, she is spattering green bile and red blood into the clean smell of a crisp uniform

and descends into darkness without a consent of the will.

First there are the drugs and sleep, the rising and falling in consciousness, subliminally aware of the patient women tending her body, turning it, feeding it liquid through little tubes, she hears fragments of conversations and loses them. She lies, unmoving, between sheets that smell of hospital bleach and soap, in a fluctuating euphoria, away from the pain

but she is fighting, wanting to be herself under any conditions, even these that are the worst, she is fighting instinctively, trying to fill out her body again, trying to be . . . Bettina. . . .

There was a party going on in the Ferrari apartment. The cigarette smoke rose slowly through the hanging plants to the high white ceilings. A young man was sitting beside her on the enormous pale green velvet sofa. His name was Stefano, and he was wearing pants so tight that they outlined his sexual organs. She was tremendously aware of that and angry with herself for falling into his trap. He was probably one of those young Italians she'd heard about who lightly sandpaper that area of their jeans so that the worn pushing look is emphasized. Stefano wore a clinging black silk shirt open to the waist and a heavy gold cross hanging on a thick chain down into the exposed hair on his chest. After all Christ died for him.

* * *

Stefano had been drinking too much and so had she and she hated it, hated the exaggeration it caused in her. She moved slowly, with enormous deliberation, putting her drink down on the table beside the sofa.

Across the room filled with people, Piero's mother, Ina Ferrari, was asking Bettina's mother pleasantly, "So you have a *palazzo* in the country, Laura?" It was a miracle Bettina could hear the question through the roar of voices and laughter in the room. She didn't hear the answer, but because she knew how to look she saw the ten years of poverty in her mother's eyes.

"And what do you do, Stefano?" she asked him abruptly.

He was pleased that she was finally talking to him, and took it for encouragement. He put his arm around her on the sofa, and leaned slightly over her, the air in his clothing flushing into her face as he did that, air warm with the heat of his body, and heavy with the scent of the lotion he had put on his skin, she could imagine his hands smoothing it on himself

and he said something foolish like, "What do I do, *signorina?* Days or nights? Let me tell you about the nights, I can assure you, the nights are more interesting than the days . . ."

She interrupted him harshly, demanding, "I mean, how do you earn your living? Surely, Stefano, you *do* earn your living?" and as he hesitated, flushed and angry, it surely was an indiscreet question to be asking a young man whose father was so very rich, she made believe she thought his hesitation in answering her was caused by a language difficulty, by her not-too-fluent Italian. She said to Piero Ferrari in English, "Please, you ask him for me in Italian. . . ." but then she didn't wait for the translation, she was telling that pretty and useless young man that she was going to be a doctor, she was studying biology, "You know biology, don't you, Stefano? You dissect animals?"

and step by step she told him what you see, what you feel in your fingertips as you dissect flesh, frog, cat, someday a human body

her voice increasing in volume, she was slashing through the witless laughter around her, she was silencing the party, her words cut perfumed flesh and disemboweled and even as she did it, she knew it was the scream of her soul trying to claw its way back into control through the pleasing devastation of the alcohol that had unhinged her.

At first she thinks it is so dark because it must be night and they want her to sleep. Even as she laboriously puts together that thought through the debilitating grip of the drugs that have been added to her blood, she knows a small fear in her belly, a tremor of understanding. The morphine is growing old and her strong young body is beginning to handle it, she is making her way into realization.

There are women somewhere nearby murmuring together. She cannot make out the words, but can catch the sibilants, like listening to a school choir singing in German, *Zu der Zeit du lezten Pasaune.* . . .

As she slowly returns, she is awakening to pain. She lies very still, groggily trying to explore its limits. At first the pain is everywhere, she is gnawed by a million small nibbling rats crawling over her. The pain intensifies, and she begins to know its boundaries: her right side is glorious, it comes out of the drug sharpening in sensation, incredibly responsive, feeling everything, the air, the heat of her own body, the fiber of the sheet, acutely alive but leveling off within normalcy.

She concentrates, sweating, on her good right side, moving her hand and foot slightly and knowing they are shifting, an agony of effort through the growing pain in her left side. At last she can ignore what's happening on that side no longer, she is mounting from level to level of pain as if she is being tested for the topmost limit she can bear. Her left side is hurt, is hurt, it was folded into the VW, she was rolled into the steel like apple into turnover.

The VW had stalled in the driving rain. She was out in the middle of the lane, pumping the starter, *ummmm, ummmm, ummmm.*

Go, will you, dammit....

Through the rain she could see headlights approaching from the other direction, coming around the curve. She kicked at the gas pedal, jamming the key in the ignition so hard toward the right that it was making her fingers go numb. The lights were on a truck, large headlights that turned into her eyes as the truck came around the curve. Her retinas were seared with the light, and for an instant all she saw was white.

She was saying to herself, thinking it was something funny, *With my luck tonight, he won't make the curve, he'll slide right into me,* and as if she were a witch summoning evil without knowing how to control it, she saw in her growingly responsive eyes the image of that truck coming sideways at her, a smooth and easy movement, not fast, not slow, simple and irresistible. She saw the truck driver high up on his seat, a heavy man in a teeshirt whipping his steering wheel around, his mouth was moving but she couldn't hear what he was saying as he came at her, and then he was gone in an enormous light that seemed to blow out of her head

and she makes herself ask the dreadful question: *Should it be this dark?*

"Oh, my God, I can't see. . . ."

She must be making a sound. She feels the movement of air as the whispering women come close to her bed. "Are you awake, Bettina?" one of them asks her. "Did you say something?"

She lies there opening and closing her eyes, so wide open she could rip the corners, so tightly closed that her eyelashes must be disappearing into the folds, and that tortures her battered face, but she doesn't notice it, for no matter what she does, the blackness does not lessen. Her heart beats wildly, she is choking with the rush of her blood, and she howls, "I can't see!"

There are hands restraining her. She must have tried to sit up, as if she could rise out of the darkness into the light. There is a slight relief in her arm as the needle comes out, and she can hear the *smack smack* of the transfusion sack swinging against the metal stand. And she repeats her scream of despair: "I can't see!"

"Get Dr. Greshak," one of the nurses is saying urgently. "He's still somewhere in the building. Hurry!" and there is the retreating scurry of rubber soles on well-waxed linoleum.

"Everything's going to be all right, Bettina," the remaining nurse murmurs. "Dr. Greshak will be here in a minute to talk to you. Shush. Shush." Bettina can feel the woman's body leaning on top of her, holding her down gently, and the "Shush, shush," continues, murmur without logic, hypnotic, trying to soothe her with sound.

Bettina lies still, her eyes wide open into darkness, the nurse on top of her. She doesn't make another sound; only her continuous swallowing makes a small squeak. After a moment the nurse draws back, patting her on the arm. "That's better, honey," she says.

"Count backwards Bettina. Ten..."
"Nine... eight..."
"Good girl. Good girl."

"Don't worry, the doctor will be right here," the nurse is saying cheerfully, and the needle slides back into Bettina's arm. She does not fight it, she does not even really feel it. She breathes fast, swallowing as if she is going to retch again, only there's nothing left for her stomach to give up.

Over the hospital loudspeaker comes the singsong announcement, "Dr. Greshak to Intensive Care. Dr. Alexander Greshak to Intensive Care..." and she knows that's for her and is scared. The sweat bells on her lip, it rolls into her mouth, she tastes the salt of fear.

She was alone. Her brother Greg had brought her to the place where the pipe of the storm drainage system exited into a local stream with an excited story about treasure far inside where it was too narrow for him to crawl. After she went into the pipe, she could see him standing at the end peering in at her, a fattish boy of ten in Cub Scout shorts and an old tee-shirt that said COLUMBIA because their father had gone to college there. Greg was calling to here, "Go on, scaredy-cat, go on, a little further, can't you see it?"

She was lighting her way down the pipe with a book of matches Greg had given her. Ahead of her she could see puddles of striped light collected under the gratings at the street corners, but the blocks were long and the distances between the puddles very dark. It was growing late and the black stripes seemed to be seeping into the light stripes, the light was slowly going out

and Greg was urging her on angrily, "Oh, for Pete's sake, can't you do anything right?"

* * *

and because she didn't want him to think she was dumb, because she wanted him to continue to include her in his adventures, she crawled on through the trickle of water, her kneecaps sore, her heartbeat suffocating her. The matches wouldn't burn because her hands were wet; finally there weren't any left, she had dropped them one by one like Hansel leaving a trail, only nobody was ever going to find them here. When the last one was used up she found herself in complete darkness, no more light anywhere or any treasure, she was submerged in black, and when she turned to look back, she saw that it was dark outside too, now, and Greg was gone, he had played a trick on her

and afterwards their mother punished him, he had to go to bed after supper for a week for doing such a cruel thing to his little sister

* * *

but for now she was alone in a tunnel under the earth

buried alive

too scared to make a sound.

There are wires in her mouth, pushing some of her teeth back into her jaw, she can feel them with her tongue. *Oh God. Oh God.* She runs the shaking flat of her right foot against her left leg, finding a tremendous cast, and her heart plunges. How much is left of flesh and bone, how much of a leg is there inside the plaster? And her arm, does she have any left arm at all?

"Stop moving around," says the nurse, grabbing her leg. "You're not supposed to be moving around."

"Okay, what's going on here?" asks a man's voice.

"Doctor, she's been thrashing around like a maniac."

"Wouldn't you, if you woke up in this condition? Let go of her, Miss DiMarco."

There is the rub of metal across the floor, a chair coming to the side of the bed, and the puff of exhaled breath as the doctor sits on it, the puff of obesity and age. "Hello, Bettina," he says. "I'm Dr. Greshak."

"Please, is there an arm?" she whispers.

"What? Oh, yes, there's an arm. Not in the greatest shape, but all there. The leg, too. Plus a few extra pieces of metal nature didn't provide, but nothing missing."

"Except . . . the eyesight. . . ."

She feels the air moving on her eyeballs as he passes his hand in front of her open eyes. "No go, huh? Well, it's what I expected, from those x-rays. But listen, you're not to give up yet. When you're stronger, we'll get a good man in to try some corrective surgery."

"Try . . ." She understands the desolation of that verb, and wants to cry, to scream, to spit, but she hasn't the strength or the heart for anger. She feels herself coming out of the other side of the morphine that was protecting her, and is being overcome by the enormity of her pain, her body throbs everywhere. Even her unwounded right side responds to the devastation of what has happened to the left side, her skin so supersensitive that she can feel the threads of the sheet scratching the good flesh

agony more acute than when she lay in the crumpled VW with the firemen torching away the metal she slides slowly backwards into the roaring pain, barely able to hear any longer

the bed trembles and her sick stomach responds, retching miserably.

She can tell that Dr. Greshak is ordering something for her. "I don't want any more drugs," she says with effort. He doesn't hear her and she has to repeat it, panting, "No drugs!"

"Time enough to be brave later, young lady," he tells her sharply.

There is an unbelievable heat in all of her body, she's burning up, her whole body is pouring sweat. Then she feels the pinprick in her arm and a delicate suffusion of cool relief moves outwards from the point of entry like undulating waves around a dropped rock, a light and beautiful sensation that sucks up the pain as it passes through, digests it, annihilates it. She finds herself exhaling, a continuous breath going out of her lungs, it seems to her she has been holding her breath forever.

"Look," the unseen Dr. Greshak is saying. "Before you go to sleep, I'm going to send in your brother and your roommate. They've been sitting out in that waiting room all night, going through hell. They won't leave until they've had a peek at you. Just for a minute, okay?"

The pain is beginning to ricochet soft and dreamlike within the distant back of her head, a slow-motion movie with the sound turned off. Even as the pain fades she knows a dull terror: The morphine will wear off and she will have to face reality again. And again.

"Bettina?" she hears Dr. Greshak insisting. "Is it okay if they come on in?"

He is poking memory through the morphine. Her brother Greg... and dear old Hoss....

and then she is thinking of Piero....

It was dawn. Mist hung on the Italian city of Florence like fairy cloth; the old buildings poked up into it and disappeared. It was thicker over the Arno River, as if the waters were exhaling gray breath. They could see an old man sitting unmoving in a small boat, fishing in the fog. He had fallen asleep with his stick in his hands, and his boat turned slowly in the flow of the river that was carrying him away. Then a steady thumping sound came from the direction of Pontevecchio, a young man sculling steadily emerged from under the bridge, his body leaning forward and backward in rhythmic movements as even as those of a machine piston. He passed the old man in the rowboat, but neither saw the other.

Bettina and Piero were jogging along the Arno. Piero was wearing a dark blue sweat suit with the symbol of Florence embroidered in gold on the breast pocket. Later his mother would tell Bettina he was the province champion in five thousand meters, but the girl didn't know that then. She had been a member of the girls' track team in high school and had confidence in herself, she knew how to run and enjoyed the movement of her legs matching his strides. She was young, she was strong, and it seemed to her they could run like this forever.

There was almost no traffic yet on the boulevard Lungarno; where the sidewalk narrowed, they went down into the street without breaking stride, and the few early-morning cars flowing past swerved tolerantly to let them continue in their path, some of the men behind the wheels turning to wave encouragement to them.

Now they were passing the end of Pontevecchio. The fancy shops on the bridge where later tourists would cluster like bees hanging on the hive were still boarded up for the night. There were young people curled up in blankets leaning on one another in small piles in the shelter of the buildings, still asleep, but stirring restlessly in the dampness that had deposited silver droplets like cobwebs on their blankets.

Piero and Bettina turned down the long narrow square past the Uffizi. Great men turned to marble along the front of the building peered out of the mist at them going by. "Where are the women?" Bettina called to them. They would not admit their guilt; they made believe they did not hear her, staring pensively ahead, concerned with their own greatness, until the young runners had gone by.

In the Piazza delle Signorie, Bettina swerved to reach up and touch the toe of the cast of the David in front of Palazzo Vecchio. Their feet striking the cobbles of the square as they ran frightened the early-morning pigeons picking in the cracks for food dropped by yesterday's tourists. The birds rose with snapping wings about the joggers, it was as if Piero and Bettina were falling through a churning river of birds. Beyond the elegant shops along Via Calzolaio the bell was tolling in Giotto's *campanile.*

They had been running too long in air thin with mist. Bettina could feel her breath gasping in her lungs, and her feet were beginning to stumble on the uneven pavement. She would not let Piero know she was weakening, and clenched her teeth so that he would not hear the wheeze of her breath. They turned down a side street away from the square, a narrow Renaissance alley with ordinary little stores on it. She could see a small hand wagon that had been left blocking the street while its owner bargained noisily somewhere out of sight with a shopkeeper. There were fresh beautiful unreal vegetables packed firmly together in the cart, cloudy-leaved cabbages, unfamiliar small-leaf lettuces, large meaty red and green peppers shiny as wax reproductions, tomatoes with pointed ends. The young joggers reached the cart, leaping over it and running on.

Bettina's trembling knees no longer would obey her will and she fell into an old bicycle chained to a lamppost. Piero pulled her to her feet, examining her anxiously to see if she were hurt. She hit his hands away, gasping, "Damn you, Piero Ferrari... damn you...." and he laughed....

They started slowly back. Her knees were collapsing under her. Piero had his arm around her waist and was half-carrying her, murmuring exultantly to her, "That was fantastic. I've never had a run like that. Never in my whole life."

Now they could hear the squeak of a heavy, slow-moving vehicle catching up to them, in an instant it would run them down. There was an old man in a top hat with a flower in the brim ribbon driving his lumbering horse-drawn carriage along the narrow street, on his way to his place in the square to serve the day's tourists. Piero pulled Bettina to one side to let the carriage pass, and then changed his mind and hailed it and they climbed aboard.

As they rode, morning arrived in Florence. Small Italian cars with honking horns began to skitter past them down the alley, impatient with the slow old carriage, swerving around it, scraping the heavy hubs of the thick wheels and rattling the bells the old man had tied to the harness of his balding horse. The old man yelled after them, "Have an accident! Have an accident!"

As the carriage passed below, women in the apartments over the shops were folding back the heavy shutters on the windows, and then leaning out to water bright geraniums in pots on the small balconies, the excess water falling to the street in a cascade of drops that caught the sunlight. In the street, old streetsweepers with brooms of twigs were spilling water out of pails onto the sidewalks, washing away yesterday's dog defecation, the pavement was dark and shiny.

Pink sunlight began to disperse the gray mist. It shone on the wonderful wooden doors of the buildings and flashed off the intriguing grotesque beautiful door-knockers: lion's heads, clasped hands, gargoyles, dragons, old men. Bettina lay back on Piero's arm in the carriage behind the clop-clopping old horse and the sun caught on the well-polished brass and flashed into her eyes. Suddenly she couldn't bear it any more. She reached her arms up into the warm air for the whole world, crying out exultantly, "Oh God! I never want to be dead!"

"Piero's not to know."
"What? What did you say, Bettina?"
"Please, Greg. Don't let Piero know."
"Bettina! What are you saying?"
She is retreating within her body again, her consciousness is being diminished by the drugs. The growing shell about her isn't responding well to her weakening control, she must hurry. "Please, Greg... promise me...."
"My God, Bettina, he's got the right to know. He's the guy who's going to marry you."
"Greg... Greg..."
She is pierced with anguish. She still sees Piero's face in that Florentine dawn, and the movement of his beautiful strong athlete's body. Oh God, she can't do this to him. She lifts her arm, trailing the tube attached to it, flailing the air weakly, trying to catch hold of her

brother's body. He grabs her hand and squeezes it, harder than he realizes, he is twisting her fingers together. She welcomes the small discomfort that pinpoints reality, whispering, "I don't want him to see me like this."

"Jesus Christ, Bettina! We're not talking about your Friday night date and a hairdo gone wrong. We're talking about Piero Ferrari. Piero Ferrari! That guy's crazy nuts in love with you."

"He shouldn't have to prove it."

"He's going to be your husband, he has the right to know. You can't keep something like this a secret from him."

"There'll be time enough to tell him later. Please, Greg . . . do it my way . . . please . . . I can't fight you now. . . ."

He gives in angrily. "Okay, okay, don't get excited. We'll argue over it later."

She remembers her roommate, Hoss, and makes a tremendous effort not to give in completely to the morphine and slip beyond the rim down into the hole. She licks her lips with her tongue to force continuing consciousness, and murmurs, "Poor Hoss. I'm sorry to do this to you."

"Well, I must admit it wasn't exactly my idea of fun time," says Hoss's familiar brusque voice, trying to make the whole thing into a half-joke, but it has been too long a night for her and Greg, and her voice is trembling. She and Greg are so hyped by their own adrenalin that they keep talking even when Bettina has descended into a lower level of consciousness and can barely follow their words.

When Bettina left Greg's apartment in search of birthday candles for his surprise party, Hoss remained in the kitchen shredding the lettuce they had brought on the bus with them from New York City. She salted and peppered the steak and set it on the broiler pan, ready to go under the flame. Afterwards, waiting for Bettina's return, she set the table for three, and since Bettina still had not come back, she idly set about straightening up Greg's sloppy bachelor apartment, there were beer cans on the floor next to the chair in front of the TV set, dirty underwear on the floors, newspapers, socks.

Someone knocked at the door, Miss Moss, the elderly landlady from downstairs, bringing with her the odor of mildew and the indeterminate number of cats she owned. Miss Moss was carrying a wrinkled white bag containing buns that once had sugar crumbs on top, but had been handled so much that the crumbs now lay in the bottom of the bag. "A little something for the birthday party," she said. What the hell.

Hoss invited her in and set another place.

Hoss was beginning to be disturbed at how long it was taking Bettina to get back, but was not really worried yet because there were logical reasons why she could be delayed. Then Greg came in from work, surprised to find the ladies in his apartment and delighted at the attention, but a little embarrassed about his housekeeping, he rushed through the rooms grabbing things and shoving them under the furniture.

They all had a glass of wine, deliberately not talking about how long it was taking Bettina to get back. Finally, it had been too long a time. Greg and Hoss went to the window, looking through the falling rain for some sign of the little red VW. "I suppose I could go and look for her," Greg said. "She probably went down to Norton's."

"Maybe you should, just so we can stop worrying."

"There's an awful tie-up just beyond that shopping center. There was some kind of an accident, I could barely get through on my way home. It must have been a beauty, there were fire trucks and ambulances. . . ."

Suddenly realized possibility clotted the voice in his throat. Hoss opened her mouth and closed it again, and the two of them ran for the door, leaving old Miss Moss still talking to nobody in particular.

They weren't able to stop anywhere near the accident. Policemen in heavy raincoats waved them on with flashlights, keep moving, keep moving. Finally Greg parked his car at the back end of the Norton's shopping center parking lot and he and Hoss ran through the rain back up the street.

The whole area was teeming with wreckers, ambulances, fire engines, police cars parked at random on the sidewalk, and everywhere there were people, they came with umbrellas and newspapers held over their heads, silently watching. Greg and Hoss pushed their way desperately into the crowd, trying to see. Some of the people let them pass without question; others resented them and would not move, "Who the hell do you think you are anyway, we was here first."

The truck that had been involved in the accident was pulled up on the wrong side of the street. It was a private garbage truck with some damage to the front fender, but looked almost untouched. The driver stood beside it with rain plastering his teeshirt to his body, smoking a cigarette, not looking at anything. He moved his mouth, but without sound. Then he threw away the cigarette and lit another and mur-

mured again.

Beyond the heads of the spectators, Greg and Hoss could see the sparks of the firemen's torches, cutting metal. Greg grabbed hold of a passing policeman. "Is that a red VW? My sister is driving a red VW...."

The policeman glanced at them sharply. "You better take a look," he said, and began to push through the onlookers, saying, "Step aside, please. Let us through."

Greg and Hoss followed him slowly. They didn't want to take a look. There was nothing they ever did in their whole lives that cost them more courage. The young policeman was clearing a space for them to pass. They had to go.

Suddenly they were looking at the wrecked car, a red VW. The whole left side was stoved in. Two firemen with torches were slowly cutting away the door. Through the glassless windshield, now pushed almost back to the seat, they could see a lumpy shape. It was impossible to tell what the clothing was like, the figure was now covered with blood.

They stood in the harsh light from the police arc lamps, numb, cold, wet, knowing it was Bettina, sure she was dead. Hoss clutched Greg so tightly that they were both bruised. Then the firemen lifted the door of the car away from

Bettina's body, and there was the joyful cry, "She's alive, she's alive...." The crowd stirred with relief, echoing, "She's alive!" as if the continuation of life must always be a blessing, life at any price. Bettina was lifted onto the ambulance stretcher. The only way Greg and Hoss were sure it was she was because of the length of the bloody hair.

They spent the night in the hospital waiting room. "What is the religious affiliation of your sister?" the admitting nurse had asked discreetly when they came in the ambulance. Shortly afterward a tall thin young priest with a black beard had run past them and pushed through the doors to the emergency room where Bettina had been brought. Later the priest, Father Sebastiano, returned to the waiting room and sat with them, talking to them about baseball and politics and ecology, and when they seemed to need it, not talking at all.

"Go on home, Father," Greg had said, several times. "We'll be okay."

"In a minute," said Father Sebastiano. "In a minute." But he did not go.

All night long doctors passed through the waiting room, men half asleep, haphazardly dressed, on their way to the operating room where Bettina had been transferred. "Take it as a good sign," the priest said earnestly. "If she were dead, I'd be the one they'd call."

It was a night of lifetimes. The truck driver who had run into the VW came at 3 AM. His night had been haunted by flashbacks of that hellish instant of impact, and he couldn't sleep. Finally his wife had said to him, "Hank, for God's sake, go on down to the hospital and find out for yourself how she is," and that was why he had come.

"I couldn't stop," he told Greg and Hoss again and again as he sat there. "I tried, God knows I tried, I turned them wheels as hard as I could but the tires slid, I couldn't do nothing." He was desperate for forgiveness.

They gave it to him: "It was that damned rain," said Greg distractedly, and Father Sebastiano added, "It's a wonder there aren't more people being brought into this place tonight, that was a real killer rain."

Finally, the man let himself accept it. "Damned rain," he repeated. He was angry as he left. "There wasn't nothing anybody could do in that rain," he said. Damned rain. Damned God.

It got to be 7 AM and the hospital crews changed, nurses, orderlies, cleaning women. Somehow, the word had already gone around about Bettina. Almost everyone walking through the waiting room called to Greg and Hoss in passing, "Any news of that little girl who's getting married?"

She was sitting on the floor of her dorm room, cutting out her wedding dress. The material was an extraordinary silk she had found, after much searching, in a small ugly shop downtown. Even the store owner had been surprised at how beautiful it was. She had unwound the dingy outside layer of the bolt under the harsh fluorescent light and inside was this gossamer. "Take it all and I give you a special price, I want you should be happy," said the shopkeeper with a magnanimous outspreading of his hands. She had ridden back to Barnard College on the subway clutching the bolt with both arms, almost not daring to look at it in the reality of daylight for fear it would really be tawdry. But it wasn't. It clung to her hands as she worked, it floated in the air as she let go.

* * *

There was sunlight coming in at the dorm window of this room she shared with Hoss, brilliant sunlight warm as flesh on her bare hands, spotlighting the white silk so that it seemed luminous. The door to the hall was open and girls passing came to sit on the beds, passing around the art book with the picture of Botticelli's *Primavera*, looking at the dress Bettina was copying.

"You're getting married in transparent veils with your boobs hanging out?" one of the girls said. "I always thought you were kinky, Bettina Weston, but this is ridiculous."

"The central figure! The central figure!" Hoss cut in impatiently.

For weeks Bettina had been haunted by the knowledge that the central altar of the Duomo of Florence had been reserved for the wedding, that the people who would turn to watch her walk to Piero Ferrari would be the most elegant, the most cruelly critical in Italy. She had tried New York City's equivalent route: accompanied by Hoss, she had sat through half a dozen wedding fashion shows with models parading their bones in expensive gowns with unreal price tags. At one place an effeminate consultant insisted angrily, "I must do the entire wedding! It must be *styled!*" Then there were the phony gasps of delight from the salesgirls as Bettina tried on costumes. The whole experience was so alien to her nature, and she hated it so much that she wasn't sleeping at night.

Then there was the divine moment of discovery during one of the lectures in Italian Renaissance painting 101 when the *Primavera* was flashed on the screen and she knew, *this is it*, the *Primavera* dress and a garland of white roses in her hair. Let Ina Ferrari's fancy friends stare at her, she knew she was right, for she was marrying a Florentine. . . .

* * *

"A dress like this should be sewn by hand," one of the girls on Hoss's bed was saying. "Completely done by hand, like it would have been done in the Renaissance. All little handmade stitches."

"Hey, I'll help you do it," offered another, and another, they sat there on the beds in the Barnard dorm in their Adidas sneakers and divided the work among them.

She is swallowing, coming awake. Somebody has been talking to her. Greg? Yes. And Hoss. When was that?

A nurse has strapped a blood-pressure band to her arm and is pumping the bulb, she can feel the tightening around her arm, that is what has wakened her. And she is uneasy, not quite remembering what's wrong with her.

"It's a Botticelli dress," she murmurs.

"What did you say, honey?" the nurse asks her.

She doesn't repeat it. She is blocking away

now with then.

The door had closed on the last of Piero's friends, the party was finally over. The beautiful room lay ugly with cigarette smoke and dirty glasses and bits of discarded food dropped into the exquisite plants and furniture.

She could see that Piero was putting a record on the stereo. "Never mind, Bettina, Gelsemina will clean in the morning," he said without looking up.

Bettina hastily put down the monogrammed paper napkin with which she had been mopping up a spill on the antique end table. It said something about her and her lifestyle that she had forgotten about the Ferraris' maid. The record started, a sensuous popular song in which a young male singer half-whispered, *"Amami . . . amami . . ."* love me, love me. Piero held out his arms and she went into them.

* * *

Wrap-around dancing in the dimly lit gymnasium at eighth grade dances and her mother making her come home early... she was intoxicated with him, she felt a tremble everywhere her flesh touched him... they had danced out onto the balcony beyond the open French doors, all of Florence sleeping beyond the Arno at their feet... and who was clutching more frantically, was it he or was it she?

The exquisite white dress she wore had been bought for her by Ina Ferrari because the clothing the Westons had brought to Italy had been too modest for this kind of a party. She had been humiliated and angered by the gift even though it was presented with Italian courtesy that apologized for the embarrassment caused the mother and daughter by forcing them into a social position for which they had not been prepared. It was only the knowing that she would be punishing Piero by insisting on wearing the clothes she had earned for herself that made her accept it, and when she saw how it made her look, she was compromised by pleasure.

"Marry me, Bettina," he said then. "Marry me."

The stars of the night came falling down into the black Arno below. She saw the light from inside the apartment shining on his face, and as they continued to turn as they danced, his face was dark and then light again, it was as if there were a lamp coming on and off within him.

"Bettina?" he insisted. "Did you hear me?"

"You're crazy," she whispered. "Tell me you're kidding," but he answered her, "I'm not kidding."

* * *

She drowned in an unfamiliar sea of emotion, fighting it. After all they'd known each other only a few days, they came from incredibly different worlds, they were too young to be serious....

He stopped her with the question that was the answer: "Do you not believe that you could love me?" and he drew her closer in his arms, pressing her into him, whispering, "Marry me, Bettina, marry me...."

amami amami

and she felt in her forehead the wild heartbeat in his throat.

"Easy, Bettina. Easy. You sure are restless tonight. What's the matter, are you in a lot of pain? Wait, I'll get something, doctor's left orders for you."

"I don't want anything," whispers Bettina. How can she explain her pain. "Please, don't give me anything."

She feels the needle going into her arm. "I hate this," she says. "I hate it. . . ." the being drugged out of consciousness, the pain, the needles, the transfusions, the catheter, the cement, the darkness. . . .

"Sh, sh," murmurs Miss DiMarco. "Shush, honey. Relax. Think of something pleasant, it costs the same. Think about your fiancé." Immediately it's obvious the girl knows she's made a mistake, she hurries on cheerfully, "Or maybe, better, think of something impersonal, that's safer. Think of an abstract." She sounds very young.

"Like what?"

"Oh, I don't know. Some fun idea. Think of a word association, like a color, maybe. Red. Think of red. What can you think of that's red?"

Blood is red, damn you. Pain is red. Despair is red. Hell is red.

". . . and twilight . . ." she can hear Miss DiMarco saying. ". . . and apples . . . and little girls' ribbons . . ."

Bettina puts her good hand out slowly to the kind stranger who is trying so hard for her, hanging on to the warm hand that answers her, forcing herself to play the desperate game

and red is the color of my hat. . . .

* * *

a bright red plastic hat with even white stitches going around the brim. She had stuck a pin of a small beetle to the crown. People's eyes always focussed on the beetle when she wore the hat, but it made her hat individual, unlike the hundreds of such hats that had been bought by other girls, it was hers, Bettina's. . . .

"Stop fighting, Bettina," calls Miss DiMarco from far away. "Relax. Let yourself go. Give yourself a break." But Miss DiMarco doesn't understand. She doesn't know that sometimes it's worth knowing the pain to know.

Bettina sat on her mother's suitcase on the windy platform of the railroad station in Florence. They were waiting for Ina Ferrari's son Piero to come and pick them up, but he was late. The hat was to be the point of their recognition. "Blue jeans and backpack and red plastic rainhat?" Ina Ferrari had said, repeating the description on the telephone. "You see, *cara*," her mother had said afterwards, "you really are dressed too informally, this is Italy," and Bettina had answered, "I don't care."

They were on their way to Laura Grimaldi Weston's native village of Montevecchio, outside Rome, the first time since she married her GI husband that she had been home. Ina Ferrari had grown up with her in the old village and they had kept up correspondence over the years. Laura Weston had deliberately planned the trip this way, coming into Milan rather than flying to Rome, so they could visit with her old friend.

The Westons had wasted precious money on first class tickets for the train from Milan because Mrs. Weston didn't want Ina Ferrari's son to see them get off a second class car. She had guessed—correctly—that her old friend had married exceedingly well.

Unfortunately, Piero Ferrari hadn't been there to see where they got off, they had been waiting in the station for quite a long time. "Do you suppose I should call Ina again and ask her about her Piero?" Mrs. Weston says.

Right then Bettina saw him running in through the entrance from the street, a slim young blond wearing narrow brown slacks and a well-cut brown leather jacket, he was looking quickly around the platform for them

and a train roared up the track from somewhere, Rome, Pisa, Bologna, there was a whirl on the platform of dust and scraps of paper and fine droplets of water and the smell of oil and Piero Ferrari raised his arm and waved to Bettina for he had seen her red hat

and he was unbelievably beautiful.

* * *

She can hear a man crying desperately somewhere. The sound rises and falls in her drugged head like waves in an endless dream of an ocean. *Poor man,* she is thinking. *Somebody must have died.* Her nostrils are filled with the antiseptic scent of this place, this damned place, this shatteringly cruel place full of death and pain, it is an anteroom to hell

> her mother's voice was whispering unevenly, "See, he's at peace at last," she saw her father's face and he was dead

She gasps and turns her head abruptly. Suddenly she can feel the bond where they have tied down her arm so that she will not disturb the intravenous again, and the annoyance of the needle in her arm, not a pain, just a reality, one of so many right now for her, every part of her seems stroked with fine sandpaper, she is extraordinarily aware of herself.

Now she hears the voices of people coming and going, their passing footsteps, the rattle of a cart, the steady *bleep* of a heart monitor. But now no one is crying but Bettina.

* * *

"You're beginning to stabilize," Dr. Greshak tells her.

"Then maybe you'll tell me exactly what my damages are."

Is he hesitating? She feels her heart beating very lightly, very fast, as if she has had a stimulant, and she says, begging, kidding, compromising, "You know I'm already adjusted to my blindness, let's have the rest of it."

"You're sure you can handle it?"

"I can handle it." But then she is not so sure.

She hears his matter-of-fact voice going down the list of her injuries, and it seems unending: the bones on her left side have been smashed almost beyond enumeration. Her severe head injury has severed her optic nerve. But what worries him the most is the fact that a sharp spear of shattered rib has pierced her kidney. Of course the repair work was done by the best man in the business, Harvey Weissmann.

She suddenly remembers that Dr. Harvey Weissmann has stopped to see her. She hadn't known who he was or that he had operated on her, he had been simply a brief presence smelling heavily of cigarettes, a passing doctor who made some kind of a remark about "You should have seen the other guy." In her preoccupation with herself she had forgotten he even exists. Now she finds out he has held her kidney in his hands.

"Okay, doc," she says. "Tell me where I go from here."

"We'll forget about the eyesight for now, that's another issue we'll face up to later. Speaking about the rest of your injuries, provided that the kidney holds, you could lead a fairly normal life. In time. But it's going to be an incredibly long road before you get to that point. To make your body work anything like it used to after this much injury to it will take months and years of therapy. It's going to be a bigger effort than anything you've ever done in your life, and it's going to hurt, it's going to hurt so much you'll think these days here in Intensive Care were a picnic."

"Oh God, doctor," she says bitterly. "Do you have any idea what I'm going through, right now?"

"I've got to tell you, kid, that if you're going to run out of courage now, I might as well forget about telling you what real therapy would cost you, because believe me it's a lot. You'd have to walk across the floor of hell to come out the other side, do you understand me? If you haven't got the guts to do that, you can always opt for a wheelchair."

There are tears sliding sideways across the exposed section of her cheek and down into the bandages around her head. She isn't a person who ever cries for herself and she fights it, closing her eyes tightly trying to stop but not able, this is a sudden unfamiliar force she cannot control. She turns her head and the small hot trickle runs down the other cheek.

"Look, Bettina," Dr. Greshak says, sounding suddenly gentle. "I think now is the time you could use your fiancé."

His murmur is insidious, sliding into her wounded soul. She imagines Piero here, she clutches him, spilling the agony from her flesh to his, she drags him down the vortex of despair with her, making him suffer because once she was someone he loved . . .

"No."

"Why not?"

It is over. She won't let it happen, not to Piero. She returns him to the Florentine Renaissance where she found him, she leaves him in her dreams.

"I think he should be here, Bettina," she can hear Dr. Greshak saying.

"I don't want him to come. Don't you see, if he comes, he'll feel he has to . . ." She stops.

"He has to what?" Dr. Greshak prompts her,

after a silence, and finally she says it out loud, "He has to . . . marry me."

"And why shouldn't he? Have you been listening to me, young lady? If you go through therapy successfully, eventually you should be quite normal again."

"*If* I go through therapy successfully. *If* I see again." She turns her head and tastes salt, it seems to her she is all over salt, as if she has just been dragged, drowning, from the sea. "I have to let him go now or he's trapped. He got engaged to somebody else. Nothing like I am now. It wouldn't be fair."

"Life is rarely fair. But it can be lived anyway."

"Don't get philosophical with me now, doctor. I'm not ready for it. Please, just accept that I don't want him to come."

"What?"

"He mustn't come."

Dr. Greshak doesn't say anything and she feels her terror growing. "You mustn't let him come. Please. I don't want him here. I don't-. . ."

She must be flailing again. Dr. Greshak has his fingers on her forehead, he is pressing so firmly that she thinks the eggshell will snap and his fingers go into her brain, she is impaled on his fingertips. "Look here, Bettina," he says strongly. "If that kidney lets go, we're in for a hell of a lot of trouble, do you hear me?"

She hears him and makes herself become quiet, enormously quiet, she hears her heartbeat slow down, disappear. After a moment he sighs and takes away his hand, but she can still feel the points where the fingers were as if they are still there.

A child dies in the next unit in Intensive Care. The child's name is Jennifer and a neighbor backing her car out of her driveway had not seen her on her tricycle behind the car. It seems at first that Jennifer is going to be all right. Her parents bring her a pull-string doll that says brightly, "My name is Debbie. What's your name?" and the child whispers, "Jennifer."

In the middle of the night, Bettina wakens to activity in the next unit. "I feel sick . . . I feel sick. . . ." the child is whimpering.

There are many subdued voices whispering; one of them is saying, "She's bleeding from the mouth," and another answers, "Oh, my God."

Bettina turns her head away, not wanting to hear. Now there's a man's voice, they've summoned the doctor on call. "Jesus Christ.

She's got to get right back on the operating table. Call Dr. Brownell. Stat. Where are the parents?"

"They went home. They were so tired, and we thought she was better."

As if she understands what they are whispering, Jennifer begins to wail, "Mommy. Please, I want Mommy. . . ."

Bettina tries to close out the sound of the frightened child. She opens and shuts her free hand, opens and shuts, concentrating so hard on that that she can feel the sweat starting under her eyes. It does no good. She begins to retch, finding the cold metal dish and holding it trembling to her mouth, not bringing up anything but shaken with sick spasms.

The child isn't crying any longer, she just makes a high-pitched sound at the top of her throat as she breathes. They are taking her away, lifting her out of the bed to the stretcher. Suddenly, the wheezing stops. After a moment they finish the business of putting the silent child on the stretcher, and quietly wheel her out of the room.

The order comes through from Dr. Greshak for Bettina to be taken out of Intensive Care. "See, honey, things are looking up," says

Miss DiMarco. "You're getting better. Doctor wouldn't be taking you out of here if you weren't."

Bettina doesn't answer. She knows what Dr. Greshak is up to. He's afraid Jennifer has left the door open.

The room to which they take Bettina faces the square in front of the hospital. She knows that because everyone who comes to the room goes to the window to watch the progress of fall. "The leaves are turning yellow," they tell her. And, "They're really magnificent this year." They don't know how unbelievably cruel they are.

Bettina isn't able to eat. Everything she manages to get down, she vomits right up again. "You're doing it to yourself," Dr. Greshak tells her angrily. "There's absolutely no physical reason why you should be vomiting up your food. What is this, a death wish?"

"I can't make myself vomit!" she yells at him. "I can't even make myself belch. It's just that my stomach is so damned tense it sends everything right back up. Why don't you give me one of your magic pills so it relaxes?"

"You're so full of relaxers already it's a wonder you don't disintegrate," rumbles the doctor. He's angry with her, he tells her, "You've got to get your head on straight, young lady. If you don't start doing better with that food pretty soon, I'm going to have to put it into your arm."

"There's no place left in the arm where you can make a hole," Bettina answers him. "The skin must look like the morning after a bedbug convention."

"My God, she's made a funny. Let's hope it means things are looking up."

The woman in the other bed in the semi-private room is a Mrs. Callaghan. Mrs. Callaghan weighs two hundred and thirty-eight pounds and has had a heart attack. Her daughter Lily brings her food smuggled into the hospital in sweaters and nightgowns.

"It's not much, really," says Lily, when Bettina murmurs something about what she's doing to the strict diet on which the hospital has put Mrs. Callaghan. "Besides, I owe her, she sneaked me pizza when I was in this place having my baby last year." The room is heavy with the smell of Chinese food.

It's a strange kind of a love, bringing food to a two hundred and thirty-eight pound woman who has just had a heart attack, but it doesn't matter to Bettina anyway. Nothing matters. Her body lives because it did not die, that's all, and living is a drifting up and down through different levels of pain.

"What's the matter, honey?"

Has she made a sound? She doesn't seem to remember it. "Nothing," she answers Mrs. Callaghan finally.

"What do you mean, nothing. You don't cry for nothing."

Damn. When you're blind you lose half the symptoms of crying, you don't even know you're doing it, there's no vision to blur, nothing but the sensation of the tears moving down your face. They must show in that light everyone insists on keeping lit at the head of her bed, she can feel its heat but it does not light up anything for her, it just shows Mrs. Callaghan the tears that have escaped.

"Hey," says Mrs. Callaghan heartily, insisting her good humor. "You've got to look at the positive side of all this, honey. We're still alive, ain't we? We could of both been in our boxes, but we're not. The good Lord's still got plans for us, He's got plans for you and me, you can bank on it."

"What the good Lord's got is one hundred and thirteen pounds of fertilizer, right here in this bed."

"Jesus Mary and Joseph. Don't even joke like that."

"Why not? The Lord must have a great sense of humor. He could have had one hell of a doctor, one who meant to do something good for Him. Now He's got nothing. Nothing. There has to be a joke there somewhere. Why aren't you laughing?"

"Oh, Bettina . . ." The voice is unhappy, confused. Bettina has hit into the soft area of the woman's soul, the unprotectable area of pure faith.

"Forget it, I'm sorry," Bettina murmurs. She is fighting Mrs. Callaghan because the woman is a fragment of God, she wants to hurt her because she still believes in the whole. *Oh, I shouldn't be causing pain because I am betrayed by Mrs. Callaghan's God.* But Bettina wants to strike out at Him, *Have at Thee, Sir God . . .* to hit with an ax the plaster saints in the churches the Mrs. Callaghans have built, to see the smiling painted heads fly up in the air, to hear the squeal of the comfortable people lighting candles to a comfortable God

who has nothing to do with her, Bettina Weston.

Greg comes whenever he is free. They try to kid each other, as if this is still the game they've always played, only somebody has thought up an extra rule or two to make it more of a challenge.

"You're not to get excited, Bets, but I called Piero."

"Oh, Greg. You promised."

"Take it easy. I told him you didn't want him to come. I had to call him because I couldn't get hold of Mom, she's out of Florence somewhere with Renato. The Ferraris are trying to locate her."

She should be thinking about her mother, but it is Piero she sees in her darkness. "How did he sound?"

"What do you think? It blew his mind. He really wants to be here, Bets. He could come in a few hours." Then he stops. Greg no longer fights her, but a silence sits between them, an unfinished silence. Something more must be said.

"You must tell him . . . he's to finish school. I want him to go on with his life." She can't continue.

"Okay," says Greg gruffly after a moment. "I'll tell him."

The rope is cut. She had to do it, but it leaves her adrift. After Greg goes, she thinks disconsolately, *If only I had really let him go that day beside the Arno. That way I'd have a little distance between us, now, there'd be some scab on the wound....*

She could see Piero running toward her with flowers in his arms. She was standing across the street from the Ferrari apartment on the bank of the Arno, and for the first time since she came to Florence she wasn't wearing something to look pretty for Piero, she had on her old jeans and a teeshirt.

He didn't notice this at first. He came to her with delight in his eyes, giving her the flowers and telling her, "The shops weren't open yet, but I told the shopkeeper that I must have flowers for the girl who is going to marry me, and he opened his door for me...." and he had brought her pink roses....

She told him then. She had to tell him. She had spent a night of agony, thinking, thinking about the rest of her life, and what it would mean to her to be married to him. This was a moment of devastating pain, standing here with her arms filled with his roses, seeing him looking at her through the netting of their perfume, his mouth slightly open as he listened, she could see the growing suffering intensifying in his marvelous gray eyes.

She was almost incoherent as she tried to explain to him what she thought, why she could not marry him: she could not be what women had been for so many centuries, simply the ornament on the arm of an active man. No matter how much she loved him, marriage to him would be an envelope sealing her in. He was studying for a career in government, and being the wife of an Italian government official would be a life for her on a social scale for which she was not prepared, and which she did not want, she would be simply an Ina Ferrari in a designer dress, living to reinforce his work, and nothing more.

* * *

Could he understand what she was saying to him? That wasn't enough for her, standing with her face shadowed by his between hers and the light. She had to stand in the light herself. For all of her life she had wanted to be a doctor, the best she could manage to be, producing, a unit standing alone.

His intellect tried to understand what she said, but his Italian soul was not ready for it yet. Desperate, losing, he asked her angrily if what she wanted was that women's liberation, like those stupid women seizing the cathedral in Milan?

She cried out at that, for it showed how little he comprehended what was most important to her. What he saw was the small exterior twitch of the enormous interior pain, he was not understanding her need to be, to *be*. "Ask me for something easy, Piero," she told him. "Ask me to slit my wrists. Ask me to sleep with you.

Don't ask me for the rest of my life, your way."

He did not give up easily. He caressed her frantically, his voice wavering as he asked her, "Is what you're saying that you don't love me enough? Is that it? I have been mistaken and you do not love me enough?"

and she cried out passionately, "God, Piero Ferrari, can't you see, that's not the issue at all, I love you so much I could throw up...."

and she groans and turns her battered face into her pillow, stifling her breath, because if that had been the end, now there would have been layers of time like sheets of insulating paper inserted between her and Piero Ferrari.

She dreams a kiss. Piero is kissing her gently, whispering, *Poverina... poverina...* my poor little one . . .

Oh, Piero. I did such a dumb thing.
What was that?
I got myself killed.
No. No. You are alive, and I am here. I am here with you . . .

It is so real that she comes awake retaining the sensation of his mouth; she thinks he is actually in the room, it seems to her that she can smell his after-shave lotion. She hears the excited reassurances of Mrs. Callaghan and Greg and Lily through her own screams. Greg is trying to get her to lie down again, he's physically pushing her down. "Piero's here!" she screams. "I can smell his aftershave lotion!"

"What you're smelling are his flowers, Bets. He's been sending them by the truckload."

"Yeah, the place looks like a goddamned funeral parlor."

Mrs. Callaghan's phrase is so ill-advised it catches Bettina's attention through her hysteria. "It was just a dream," Greg tells her. "It was just a dream." She no longer thinks she can smell Piero's after-shave lotion, what she smells is roses, she is buried in roses. Slowly, she grows calm.

"Oh, Bets," her brother tells her sadly. "You want him so badly you think he's here.

Don't you think you ought to reconsider?"

and she yells at him, "No!"

The floor nurse is at the door. Bettina's screams have reached her at her station down the hall, and she clears the room of visitors. Greg and Lily go, and the two patients are left alone together to share the experience of their failed bodies.

"How about a little TV, honey?" Mrs. Callaghan says, thumb poking at the button of the switch.

Bettina doesn't say anything. Mrs. Callaghan constantly forgets what a half-experience TV is for someone who is blind. Anyway, she is completely overwhelmed with weariness, it seems to her she has never been this tired in all her life, not after a track-meet, not after a double shift of waitressing on the weekends at Willard's Pancake House. Suddenly, she has nothing left, no resource of courage.

She can hear the clicking of the TV switch, the passing fragments of programs being tried out and rejected. Do TV producers know that patients suffering in hospitals watch their products? Do they care?

Mrs. Callaghan asks no questions about what is offered. She settles upon a situation comedy with canned laughter where it is supposed to be funny ("It ain't much, but it's just about all that's on, honey") and submits herself to an hour of mediocrity, gives away an hour of her life . . . and an hour of Bettina's. . . .

Oh God, oh God, how easy living is for some people, to come through a heart attack that nearly killed her, to come back to life and not be any different, not to have changed at all, not to have to speculate, or to put different values on the uses of time, the canned laugh is just as engrossing, just as important, as the act of dying.

". . . no more static cling . . ." says the TV and Mrs. Callaghan goes along with it. "That's good stuff, it really works. Did you ever try it, Bettina?"

Bettina does not answer. Static cling. Bad breath. Scented toilet paper. Super-shining floors. Towels that smell fresh. Blue water in the toilet. And the world is full of children growing up without food, brain-damaged forever, or growing up not knowing how to read, how to fill out a job application, growing up never having heard Beethoven, or Shakespeare.

She is restless with this good American woman who has cold hard plastic covers on her sofa, has soda and beer and potato chips delivered to her door, has fifty dollars put away for a high funeral Mass to be sung for herself, she isn't going to go into the ground accompanied by "Jesus Christ Superstar" on the guitar, has sad answers to everything and doesn't realize they're sad, and no questions

and how easy it is to live that way, how beautifully temptingly easy to lose oneself in such a world, a minute-by-minute life, there can be no pain in such a trivial world, no real pain.

Bettina's Barnard roommate Hoss comes in on the weekend to see her. "You shouldn't be here," Bettina says. "Somebody's going to get our beer."

"Let 'em have it," says Hoss. "It's no fun drinking alone."

There was always a sixpack in the little refrigerator of Bettina's dorm room. It belonged to the husky Texan girl who had been assigned to be her roommate.

"The name is Mary Cartwright," the girl said. "But everyone calls me Hoss. You know, after the big guy in the old *Bonanza* show?"

* * *

"Do you mind?"

The big girl was surprised that anybody bothered to ask the question. "Mind? Hell, yes, but I understand that the coincidence is too much for the limited intelligence of the masses. It'd take more energy than I'm willing to give to fight it."

"Do you want me to call you Mary?"

"Whatever for? Nobody'd know whom you were talking to."

"I'd know. You'd know."

"By now *I* might not even know it any more."

Hoss Cartwright had a penchant for

enlarged photographs which she tacked side by side across the wall: herself aged eleven squatting down with one hand on the ground, wearing a full football uniform ("Guess what my father wanted instead of a girl. God gave me the build, He gave me the muscles, He gave me everything except the penis"), a photo autographed by all the members of the Dallas Cowboys, a poster of half-nude Mikhail Baryshnikov leaping to God, a close-up of something that looked like a lizard's eye.

Bettina had brought what was left of herself to Barnard in one suitcase. At the end of last summer, her mother had sold the small development house where Greg and Bettina grew up. For two days a bonfire had burned in the backyard vegetable garden. Sheet by sheet Bettina had fed the flames: first grade lessons marked with smiling faces, programs for school plays, the scrapbook she kept one year on the Yankees. Greg stored a few boxes of her belongings at the back of a closet in his small apartment, but Bettina watched most of her childhood rise into the sky in gray smoke. She tacked nothing at all on the dorm room walls, it was as if she came to Barnard with no past.

"Don't mind me," she told Hoss when the girl tried to be friendly. "It has nothing at all to do with you. You've just hit me at a bad time in my life."

"A guy?"

"Everything. We closed down our old life last week." She could see Hoss looking at her, waiting for more, but they were not yet good enough friends.

Bettina does not sleep well at night. When her drowsy mind is most weak and undistracted, it indulges in the sad pursuit of the other possibilities she had on the night of her accident. But she cannot rewrite what happened. The story is printed. The car stalled and the truck came across the road and hit her. That is done now, and life has gone on from that point, there's no changing any of it.

The young priest, Father Sebastiano, often turns up in the very early hours of the morning, before the hospital routine meshes into operation. She has no idea how many times he has stood in the doorway of the room and looked at her before she realized he was there and called him in.

"The dying hour is 3 AM," he tells her. He often walks the halls of the hospital at night, watching. "Well, young lady, and what's your excuse for not sleeping?"

She does not tell him. She changes the subject, just glad he is here sharing her wakefulness in this night place of uneasy sleep and sighs and efficient quiet running feet in the halls. They whisper together like conspirators in that waiting moment just before baths and breakfast and they never speak of God but they are speaking of nothing but God.

She finds herself telling him about her father. Barry Weston died when she was eight, and by now she has used up her mental image of him, she can no longer summon up his living face in her mind, she only knows the face in the photographs. What she does remember is the awful smell of the sickroom, the loud cheerful voice of the practical nurse who came every day to give him his enema. She remembers how much she loved him, how desperately she hated his death. She remembers his love story.

It was very late and she had been in bed. What was it that called her to her parents' bedroom that night, a bad dream, perhaps, a sound she could not explain, a loneliness, a premonition?

She knocked timidly at the door. Her mother was in her nightgown, sitting on the side of the cot where she now slept; Laura Weston had not been sleeping in that bed of death with her young husband for over a month, now. Ostensibly that was because she didn't want to disturb his fragile sleep, but later on, later on she would admit she could not stand the sick coldness of him, she would be torn with guilt that she had removed herself and the warmth of her healthy young body from him, she had denied him that comfort.

Thin thin Barry Weston was lying against a stack of pillows looking at his wife's smooth arms, hands to her head as she took out the pins in her long hair. He did not turn to look at Bettina as she entered the room, his eyes were filled with the look of his beautiful wife.

"What is it, Bets?" her mother asked her, and Bettina answered hesitantly, "I couldn't sleep."

"Lie in my bed while I finish combing my hair." The child gladly curled up on her mother's pillow, smelling the perfume of the shampoo from her mother's hair that had passed into the cotton pillow case. Her feet were cold; she pulled them up under her old and shabby nightgown, curling her toes within it like a turtle drawing itself into itself.

"Did I ever tell you, Bets, about the first time I saw your mother?" her father asked her.

* * *

He had told her. He had told her a hundred times. She lay drowsing on the pillow, knowing the story, loving it, it was Cinderella and Snow White and every fairy tale that ever was.

During World War II he had come, a young American captain, in the push up Italy, to the poor little town of Montevecchio, outside Rome. There were three buildings of importance in Montevecchio: the church, the mayor's *palazzo*, the home of the schoolmaster. Barry Weston had gone to the mayor's *palazzo*, and someone ran to get Laura Grimaldi, the daughter of the schoolmaster, because it was known she spoke some English. While they were waiting, the mayor had presented the young American with a glass of wine, with an obsequious little bow; Montevecchio had just been vacated by the Germans, and the people were not quite sure how they had to treat the new masters. Barry Weston, who was not used to being a conqueror, had been uncomfortable, wishing this done and himself back at the ugly honesty of war.

*   *   *

"There was sunlight coming in long shafts from the great big high windows, puddles of yellow on the floor. Your mother came walking toward me. I couldn't really see her at first because of the shafts of sunlight in the way, and then she stepped into one and she was lit up like she was in a spotlight, she was covered with light. God, was she beautiful! My heart went absolutely bingo."

When it was time for the American troops to leave Montevecchio, the girl Laura Grimaldi had stood at the crossroads alone, watching the trucks pulling out. The people of her village were sorry to see the young men leave, they passed bottles of their homemade wine into the hands of the soldiers. Some of the GIs jumped down briefly to kiss girls goodbye, with their buddies calling after them, "Hey come on, you'll get left," and the hands parted, and the men went away.

*   *   *

The jeep carrying Barry Weston had been near the end of the convoy. Laura Grimaldi spotted him and waved timidly. He stood up to look at her, turning so that he could continue to see her as the jeep went away. He did not jump down to her as the others had done, but cupped his hands to his mouth and called to her, "Wait for me, Laura. I'll be back."

"What?" she asked, not understanding what he had said, and he repeated it, in his meager Italian, to be sure she understood him, "*Aspettami, Laura, ritornerò.*" A troop truck came between them, engines roaring. The dust roiled. It began to rain, spattering mud.

Bettina was asleep before the familiar story ended. It did not matter, she knew what happened. Her mother did not carry her back to her own bed, but simply settled herself in the space remaining on the cot, next to her child. Bettina woke in the middle of the night because her mother was getting up to give her father the bedpan. She lay cuddled in the hole of warmth under the blankets where her mother had been curled around her; she was watching down a road she had never seen for the sight of her strong young father coming back at twilight to take her mother away with him on his white charger

and the bedpan made a small hollow sound as it hit the side of the bed, going under the blankets of her father's deathbed.

"Why are you doing this, Bettina?" Father Sebastiano asks her.

She knows there is no purpose to this conversation. She had hidden away the dreadful details of her father's dying in the convoluted passageways of her mind and has not allowed them daylight since they happened, but suddenly, now, in her own dreadful details, she is haunted by them. This young man is a priest and so he is vulnerable, he has to listen to her. For everyone else she is obedient and patient and simple as water, but with the priest she cracks open and pours out the blackness of her soul.

Her father died forever, for so long that finally she didn't really remember any other life. Oh, she wasn't truly aware that he was dying; the belief that children are supersensitive, super-aware, is a fantasy, they actually trust the half-truths their mothers tell them, *See, he ate a bit more today, he's doing better.* She had skipped to school and was jealous of somebody's new dress and only when she got back into the house again, into that still place full of the scent of death, did she think about her father, and then only to wonder when he was going to finish painting the outside of the house, and maybe today she'd find him in the kitchen looking in the refrigerator for the makings of a sandwich.

One day he seemed to be infused with one of those miraculous moments of strength and life the dying sometimes experience. His voice was strong, his hands didn't tremble, he put his thin feet down on the floor, saying, "Let's go for a ride." His wife wondered what the doctor would think about that, but they didn't ask him. Greg was fourteen then and skinny, but strong. He and his mother half-carried the sick man out to the car, and he had been impatient, telling them, "I can do it by myself, stop fussing with me." He had lain in the back seat of the car, on the pillows they had put there for him, and looked out of the window.

His wife and children climbed into the front seat of the car, turning to look back at the dying man. He was incredibly thin and yellow-faced, but smiling, without pain, excited at being outside again. It was like a holiday, that trip in the car. Laura Weston had driven them around the countryside, and the world had never seemed more beautiful. It was late summer, and everything had the hard bright look of summer's end, the greens were dark, the yellows golden, the fields were ripe.

"It'll be autumn, soon," said Barry

Weston, looking out at it. It would be autumn and the leaves would turn. They'd have to take another ride out to see them. Yes, they'd take another ride.

Afterwards they carried him back to his bed. He couldn't make his legs sustain the weight of his body and he had wet himself. "It is time for him to go to the hospital," the doctor told them. "You can't manage him here at home any more. Tomorrow we take him to the hospital."

Tomorrow he was dead.

"What are you trying to tell me, Bettina?"
"That there's a time to die."
"That's up to God."
"Is it?"
"Stop this, will you? Stop it. . . ."
The young priest pursues her soul down the dark alleyway where it runs. She does not stand and fight; his blows hit air and disappear with futile grunts. "People don't will themselves dead," he tells her finally.

"The Spaniards couldn't make slaves out of the Indians. They just lay down and died."

"Your father was a man with a terminal illness."

"There are all kinds of terminal illnesses, Father."

"When there are people who care...."

"Because there are people who care...."

Their fighting whispers hiss in that sad place, troubling the sleep of the good and foolish woman in the next bed, she groans and turns precipitously so that the straining wheels of her bed shifting on the waxed floor squeak slightly under her enormous weight.

They whisper more quietly, the priest bending to Bettina's ear. "You haven't the right."

She sighs and turns away from him, dismissing him. Down the hall she can hear the cheerful voice of a nurse starting another day, waking someone, "Good... morning...."

God is a very old man poking a small fire in a stone fireplace

He lets her sit curled up beside His fire because she is cold, so cold

she watches the sparks climb up the chimney and turn into stars

You are one of the chosen ones, one of the lucky ones, God is telling her. *I started you off with a perfect body.*

I know, but I had an accident. I'm all broken in pieces. I'm blind. And then, angry, she asks Him, *Why did you let it happen to me?*

He looks at her sadly. His eyes are little windows through which she can see things moving, oceans rising and falling in smooth waves, crowds of people, if she moves her head she can see sideways into the scene, she could crawl inside and run beyond the edge of the frame.

You want free will, He tells her. *You must understand that that kind of freedom leaves you free for tragedy, too*

free for tragedy

There are flowers in His long robes, and bees. She is in a line of children in a field, they are running, snapping the whip. Her feet fly out from under her, and she falls down into the soft high grass, looking upwards through the bending stalks at the blue sky wild with birds.

"Mom is coming tomorrow," Greg tells her. "I'm picking her up at JFK at 4:14 and we'll come right to the hospital. She was in Sicily with Renato. The Ferraris hired a detective to chase her down."

"Poor Mom...."

The church bells were ringing. The sudden sound of them made Laura Weston cry. "*Sù, sù,*" her mother told her. "You do not cry on your wedding day."

Bettina was sitting on the cold cement windowsill, twining daisies in her long black hair. She was watching the people coming down the road of the village toward her grandmother's house, carrying bouquets of flowers they had picked early in the morning in the fields, sunlight echoing in the drops of moisture in the petals.

"*Ciao*, Bettina!" one of the young men below called up to her, waving his arms and smiling. "Eh, come on down!" She heard him and did not hear him, for she had just fled from Florence and Piero and it was too soon for anybody else.

"Mamma, I was thinking of Barry,"

Laura Weston was saying sadly. "It was from this very room that I went to him...."

and her mother said, "It is all the will of God."

The sun was hot as they stepped out of the cool dark house. Laura Weston was wearing a long sleeveless yellow dress with embroidery on the skirt, and carried exquisite yellow roses lying across her arms. The florist from Rome had brought them early in the morning, a small excited man; it had been a long drive and his little three-wheeled delivery truck had broken down several times on his way to Montevecchio. Zio Nenni sent for a *cappuccino* for the man from the bar down the road. The little truck departed with wild flowers tied to the door handle.

Now a group of men was coming to the schoolteacher's house, Laura Grimaldi Weston's brothers, uncles, cousins. At the center was the lawyer she had met at the Ferrari apartment. Renato Caligeri was in a simple gray silk suit, an exquisite Florentine suit in the village of Montevecchio, with a small boutonniere of white flowers pinned to the lapel. He was a handsome man. The other men around him looked clumsy in contrast, peasants in their best clothes. He walked with an air, with style. He did not speak to his bride as she came out to meet him, but he looked at her. It was in that moment, in the look and the slow entwining of their arms, rather than in the ceremony later in the church, that Bettina lost her mother.

The party started down the road in that hot sunshine. Along the edge of the procession gathering as they went were men playing small trumpets and whistles, and there was a boy with a drum, beating with enthusiasm, *boom boom boom*, strong as a heartbeat. The young girls were laughing and whispering among themselves and glancing sideways at the young men walking along with the crowd going to church. The other people followed more slowly.

* * *

The road curved. Now they were passing the mayor's *palazzo*. The windows of the *palazzo* needed a washing. The wedding party was reflected in them, but dully, like a scene observed through mist. No one but Bettina turned to look at it. In that room to the right next to the central doorway, the young American captain, Barry Weston, first saw the schoolteacher's daughter, Laura Grimaldi, in the shaft of sunlight. *Bingo* . . .

They had reached the crossroads where Laura Grimaldi had stood to watch the American convoy move out toward Rome. The wedding party turned away from that road and went up the hill to the church. It was a steep climb, and they were all panting and sweating with the heat of the summer sun. The bell in the old *campanile* was swinging steadily, welcoming them, tolling an end to what had come before. Renato Caligeri smiled at his bride, taking her hand in his, and they entered the ancient church.

* * *

During the ceremony, a white pigeon fluttered down to the altar from the rafters where it had been hiding, making the children giggle, but the old people were pleased, it was like the Holy Spirit, surely, a good omen.

"I'm sorry to do this to you, Mom."
"What are you talking about? We're going to have you up in no time, *cara*."
Bettina does not answer her. She doesn't even hear the exact words her mother says, she is just listening to the bright familiar sound of her mother's cheerful voice making possible the impossible.

The milkman was knocking at the door to be paid and they had just discovered that the five dollar bill her mother thought she had hidden at the back of the kitchen drawer for emergencies was not there. They had rooted desperately through the coupons and the old half-burned birthday candles and guarantees and paper clips and left-over Christmas candy-canes, but the money was not there, it was lost or spent or never was

and Laura Weston went to the door with a smile, saying, "Well, Mr. Grover, we've had a temporary disaster, but will you have a cup of coffee on account? I really make good coffee." And Bettina covered her head with a pillow on the sofa in the next room so that she wouldn't have to listen, her stomach curled, hard, with the effort of her mother's laughter, she knew her mother was using her beauty to distract this vulnerable uncomplicated soul, giving Mr. Grover the illusion she thought him attractive, any weapon to protect her family—without shame, none—and he sat and drank the coffee and God knows what he told his wife about the unpaid bill.

"Dammit, Mom, how can you always be so cheerful?"
"What?"
Her mother has been telling her about Sicily,

about fishermen bringing in their small boats at twilight, about Roman and Greek amphitheaters side by side under the harsh white sun of Syracuse, about the purple waters where Ulysses sailed, bright sunshiny images, but a dark level below, Bettina has been hearing her mother yearning... *Renato mio... Renato....*

"You know you don't want to be here in this horrible place with me half dead, you're dying to be with that macho man of yours. And still you're being cheerful about it, you're being a good little girl...."

and even as she says it, she knows her mother will never be different, she was raised to be a good little girl, and so were her grandmother and her great-grandmother and an incredible line of little girls standing one after the other backwards into time

and all of it, all the goodness, has led to this instant, to her, Bettina, to this ugly shred of life imposed upon her that she is supposed to accept with gratitude

and she does not want it.

"Don't get excited, *cara*," she can hear her mother murmuring, her mother's hands straighten out the sheets as if it is possible to straighten out everything.

It won't be long, Mom, Bettina promises her. *It won't be long.*

"I used to bring Daddy a great big can of Prince Albert tobacco, didn't I?"

"Why, that's right, Bets. You remember that? It was a little ritual the two of you had between you, nobody else was allowed to take part in it."

Bettina feels a sudden longing for her father. "They allowed him to smoke?"

"At the end . . ."

and it was Bettina who brought him the can every night, and would sit with him while he slowly brought a few shreds of the tobacco at a time out of the can to stuff in his pipe. She would turn as he did that so that she didn't have to watch his hands, the thin waxy sick hands

"And he took yellow capsules, didn't he?"

"Yellow capsules? I don't really remember, it's been such a long time . . . oh, wait a minute, I seem to recall something. Yes, I think he did. That's right, I remember them now, those were the pain-killers. How did you know about them? They were so very powerful I was afraid of them, I tried to hide them so you children would not know they even existed. He only could have one of them at a time, they were so strong, two if the pain was unbearable. Near the end they didn't seem to have any more effect on him, the poor man could not sleep."

Suddenly, Bettina understands why her father could not sleep. The smell of that dark tobacco is exploding in her nostrils

> It was the night before he died, after their ride out into the countryside to look at the end of summer. She had brought him the can of tobacco as always, but this time he did not have the strength to pull off the tight lid. She was strong and healthy and thoughtless because everything was possible for her, and she quickly took the can away from him and yanked off the top, saying, "I can do it for you, Daddy."

> With a burst of effort, the dying man snatched the open can away from her as if it were an obscenity she must not touch. He lay afterwards on his propped-up pillows, gasping, clutching the can to him with all the waning strength in his trembling arms. In a moment he

had control of his breathing again and reached out and touched Bettina's hair with his terrible hand.

"Sorry, Bets," he said, smiling softly. "I just didn't want you to spill it all over the bed," and then he asked her to get him two glasses of water. Two! Why did he want two? and he whispered, "Why, I have a very great thirst."

And the two glasses of water were so intriguing she forgot to ask him the other question she had for him

and the two glasses stood empty on the night table in the morning when he was dead.

Oh, my God!

for the question she had wanted to ask him was why were there all those yellow capsules in the black of

the tobacco

and she only remembers it now when she understands the answer, when she realizes the long and patient hoarding of the yellow capsules that should have been bringing him relief in the dreadful night hours, hidden one by one in the tobacco she faithfully brought him in her little daughter ritual every night before she went to bed. And she knows now that that evening, after the glorious ride in the car, when the doctor had given him his sentence of going to the hospital to wait for death, he had sent her after the two glasses of water while he rooted out the capsules he had hidden, and after she had kissed him goodnight and skipped off to bed, he had fulfilled his plan

and it had taken two glasses of water, for he had a very great thirst

for death.

The slow hospital days end, visitors departing slowly. Back rubs, final medications, lights out. Bettina holds between her fingers the capsule the nurse gives her to help her sleep, gulping down a mouthful of water and saying loudly, "Okay, that's down," and afterwards, when the halls are quiet, she slowly slowly pulls out the drawer of her night stand and puts the capsule with the others in the half-empty Kleenex box at the back of the drawer behind the hand lotion and powder and candies and Piero's unopened letters. Sometimes she stirs the small hoard with her finger; they are smooth, they are medium-firm. How many will be enough? Did her father ask himself the same question? And how many angels dance on the head of a pin?

She bears the unrelieved pain at night with a secretive glee, it is her small down payment on extinction. One night the pain is too bad for her to handle; she fumbles in the Kleenex box and steals back a capsule for herself, she swallows it, sticking in her throat without water, finally sighing with the relief it brings, but anguished with her own special conception of guilt.

She can hear voices out in the hall, whispering, Dr. Greshak, her mother, others. Every once in a while she catches something.

". . . sliding into the grave . . ." They're talking about her. They know she's dying. Slow or fast, she's dying.

"Oh, please doctor . . ."

There's the squeak of the wagon carrying dinner trays down the hall. There's the distinct and somewhat unpleasant odor of peas.

"... strong ... it's been a hard life ... couldn't have gotten ... don't understand ..."

"... hard to handle ... harder for strong to accept weakness. ...

"... do something. ..."

do something

and Bettina doesn't care, she drowses peacefully and dreams of her dead father, she has not felt this close to him since he died, she shares more with him now than with any of the living, for he has shown her what the truly strong do, he has given her an inheritance to use against too-slow death.

"Look, he's very alone," Dr. Greshak is saying. "And it might do you good to think about somebody else for a while, Bettina. God, you feed on your own troubles like a maggot on diseased flesh."

"Why don't you try talking to him, *cara*," says her mother. "He's really a nice boy, and he could use a friend."

They're talking about Mischa Antonych, a sailor recently defected from the Soviet Union, who is now an orderly on Bettina's floor. She knows him only as a presence that comes and goes with a mop each morning, talking briefly to Mrs. Callaghan, who seems to think that the way to solve his obvious lack of knowledge of English is to yell a little louder. Bettina understands that Dr. Greshak and her mother are trying to make her respond to someone, anyone, in asking her to be friendly with this displaced young man; finally, because it's easier not to argue, she agrees to try to talk to him.

Oddly, as she gets to know him, she finds herself haunted by this young man. Slowly, with some guessing on her part because his English is so bad, she learns his story: he has defected from a Russian cargo ship in New York Harbor. His father is a political prisoner in the Soviet Union, and he himself escaped with difficulty through the efforts of a reluctant uncle in Moscow. A friendly refugee organization in New York has found him this job among the immigrants from many countries, most of them in the Caribbean, who staff the lower echelons of St. Mary's Hospital.

Eventually it is Mischa Antonych's incredible loneliness that penetrates Bettina's walls. His sadness, his longing for things lost, are other shades of her own colors. His heavily accented schoolboy English is almost incomprehensible, but in spite of it, she realizes that of all the people around her, only Mischa lives in her dimension of pain.

"What does he look like?" she asks Mrs. Callaghan.

Mrs. Callaghan has trouble articulating it. "Well, he's growing a beard," she says finally. "It's not that long, yet, kind of scrabby looking, like he really could use a shave. You know?"

"Blond or brunette?"

"I guess you'd call him brunette. And skinny like you wouldn't believe." She's warming up to the subject. "It's because he's so tense. With being in another country and all, I guess. Tenseness can eat you up like hamburger."

"But what does he look like?"

"You mean, is he good-looking? I think he'd be real cute if he wasn't wearing them Harold Lloyd glasses. They're all you see of his face, you know what I mean? Or is Harold Lloyd too long ago for you?"

"Mrs. Callaghan, Harold Lloyd is alive and well on the college campus."

Does Mrs. Callaghan understand that? Probably not, she's repeating herself, "Yeah, he's got these Harold Lloyd glasses. Somebody ought to tell him about contacts."

*   *   *

Rain has been falling for days. There is the feeling in the air of limpness, of lethargy, sheets are cold against the flesh. That fact, the unending rain, permeates conversation, life, the whole rhythm of the hospital. Everyone's soul is saturated with the rain.

Bettina listens to the sound the drops make, hitting the windowpane. What were the names of those two raindrops in the Christopher Robin poem that were running down the glass? John and James? That's right. *John and James are having a race. John's the one I want to win.*

Mrs. Callaghan is out of the room, walking slowly to the hall toilet with Lily. Mischa comes to clean up the mess of a dropped dinner tray. He doesn't speak to her, but Bettina is aware of him mopping between the beds, she can hear the sound of his breath as he bends. She wants to say something to him, but doesn't know what.

Piero is studying Russian, Mischa. You two probably could have quite a conversation together. He's going to be sent to Russia by his government some day. . . . It hurts too much to think about that. *Oh, dear, John is losing the race. Poor John, he will never get to go to Russia. . . .*

She feels Mischa touch her arm. "Please, miss," he says softly.

Is she crying enough for it to be noticed?

Such a stupid thing to do. With all the dreadful things in her life, she's crying real tears over two raindrops in a child's poem....

The orderly is trying to console her but he has too many echoes in his own soul. Maybe the rain has been falling for too long. He breaks down and weeps, his face in the sheets. She finds herself holding on to him, with all her limited strength. She can feel the thinness of him, all bone, through his rough uniform shirt. He doesn't smell of expensive after-shave lotion, he smells of sweat and hospital disinfectant. He is shaking with the intensity of his suddenly released emotion, he tears apart.

His grief bursts open doors for her one after the other. She knows a quick explosion of relief as she rushes out of the black corridor that has contained her, into limitless space. The tightness of her personal torture chamber disperses, dilutes, flies apart in all directions. What an exultation to cry out loud at last. What a fierce release, like flight

and so they clutch each other desperately, two souls in unsupporting space, anchoring themselves together.

"Hey, hey, Bettina. Watch out for that boy. You'll find him in your casts with you one of these days, if you're not careful."

Bettina almost cannot comprehend the

sudden voice breaking into her surrender, it cannot be the language she speaks, for it has no message for her, no pertinence, it is a tree branch squeaking randomly against a windowpane.

But it persists. It insists. It says words. "Hey, kids. Lay off, this is a hospital, you know. . . ." It makes a strange grating vibration of a laugh, Mrs. Callaghan come back from her mission of mortality.

Mischa responds first. He pulls away from Bettina, murmuring in Russian. She hears him run away.

"Was he crying?" Mrs. Callaghan asks curiously. The thought seems to bother her, she believes it's wrong for a man to cry. She is offended by Mischa's tears as if she has seen an obscenity, an exposure of a private part.

"Why shouldn't he cry?"

"It makes him look, you know, weak." It isn't a comment Mrs. Callaghan enjoys, but she feels she must say it.

Bettina turns away. Dr. Greshak would be proud of her. She is thinking about somebody else. She is thinking about the orderly who is man enough to cry.

It is late night and there's someone in the

room with her besides the snoring Mrs. Callaghan. "Father Sebastiano?" she asks softly.

"Is Mischa."

"My God, Mischa. It must be 1 AM. What are you doing up so late? Can't you sleep either?" and he answers her hesitantly, "I do not sleep so very much."

Somehow, after this afternoon, she has almost been waiting for him, and yet, though they had embraced like frantic lovers in their despair, now they are shy with each other.

He has brought her a gift, an apple from the hospital pantry, apologizing that it is not more. Everything else is locked up, frozen, unavailable to him. She knows, through common hospital knowledge, that he lives in a small windowless area in the hospital basement divided off from the laundry machines by a hanging curtain, free lodging in exchange for his availability for small repairs during the night of the heating and cooling plant.

"Is beautiful," he says. "Decoration, black and dust."

"Oh, Mischa..."

"Okay, okay. I am Russian realist. Besides, they not tell me I cannot play guitar. I play very loud, I yell songs of home. Scare washing machines. Next day, crew says, 'Hey, who's been tampering with machines?' I am very innocent. I look over shoulder, who did it?"

The apple is extremely smooth, as if it has been rubbed. "Thank you, Mischa," she whispers. There is no answer. He is gone.

She was walking slowly along the Hudson River. It was winter and twilight; the strong wind was pushing her, half-running, downtown. It was a cold wind, she wished she had worn a heavier coat, but the sensation of piercing cold delighted her. She felt as if she were finally coming alive, the tough protective layers she had built up about herself were penetrated. Suddenly, she was Pascal wearing his belt of nails to remind himself of the glory of the flesh.

She knew she was working too hard, spending too many hours in the lab and in the library; it was the way she was able to blot out speculation about what she had left behind in Florence, it was the way she was able to go to sleep at night. Sometimes when she ran up the broad marble steps to class in Milbank

Hall, she had to grab hold of the broad mable balustrade to keep from falling. But she would shake her head and run on, always looking at the world through glasses of tears.

There was almost no one at this hour on Riverside Drive, just some mothers and children already bundled in snowsuits and knit hats with pompoms. It was suppertime in New York, the wind was unpleasant, but the river was magnificent, and nothing at all like the Arno. She sat on one of the hard park benches and looked at the Hudson for a while. The waters were churning white caps in the gray; a slow-moving barge was carrying coal upstate to Albany. In a few minutes it would slide under the heroic framework of the George Washington Bridge, which was already lit up with pale green lights strung on cables against the purpling palisades of New Jersey.

Bettina was shaking with cold, but hated to leave, there was something incredible about this moment in the loneliness of cruel twilight, she seemed to be responding to the scene about her like a poet. The knowledge that she would have to return to the college with its lights and heat and girls in brightly colored witty teeshirts gave her a sense of entrapment, of loss, of telescoping down to life in a dollhouse.

But she could delay continuation of living only briefly; eventually, she had to start back. There was no one anywhere along the Drive now; the children had run off to warm apartments and hamburger suppers. The only person she could see as she walked slowly northward was a young man standing looking across the river, his body a silhouette against the Jersey shore. He was dressed completely in black, black shoes, black slacks, black hip-length jacket with black fur, and there was something about his hair in the weak pink light that made her think of her lost Piero, it stabbed her with such remembrance that she began to run

* * *

and as she passed him he turned suddenly and said clearly to her, "That is some river you have there," which was what she had said when she first saw the Arno

for he was Piero.

Fortunately there was no one else on the Drive to witness what came next, for she was hysterical, and so was he. They told each other they could manage some compromise, anything that had to be done, for they could not live apart.

But she was afraid, she asked him, "Can we make it work? Do you honestly think we can make it work?"

"*T'amo*, Bettina," he told her.

"Oh God, Piero, is love enough?"

*   *   *

"Love is enough," he told her with calm surety. She looked at him almost with fear, this protected child of privilege who had always had everything he wanted, and did he really know himself, and did she really know him . . . but in the end she was trapped by wanting him so badly

and so she believed him.

Mrs. Callaghan goes home. Her daughter gathers up the shedding flowers, the almost empty boxes of candy, the romance paperbacks. They are on their way to a roast beef dinner with the grandchildren.

Mischa brings the wheelchair, and sighing and puffing, the old woman is wedged into it. "Just a minute, boy," says Mrs. Callaghan, and stops to embrace Bettina; the girl finds herself falling into soft flesh. "Everything is going to be okay, honey," the woman says. "You wait and see."

There is a moment of silence with nothing more to say. Mrs. Callaghan squeezes Bettina's good hand and lets it go. Her voice loses its genuineness and becomes knowing again, bantering: "I'm leaving you in Mischa's hands, now. Or maybe I shouldn't say that, he might take me up on it, huh, Mischa? Be sure you behave yourself, boy. Remember she's in a weakened condition."

Oh, God.

"Well, good-bye, honey. You come see me when you get out of this rathole and we'll have a real party, you hear me? Call me, I'm in the book," and the wheelchair squeaks, taking her away.

Come see me... there's an infinity of thoughtlessness in the platitude. Bettina listens to the voices going away from her with the surety that she will never visit Mrs. Callaghan, that she will never even know anything more about her, not even the day the high Mass will be sung

within the year.

The woman who takes Mrs. Callaghan's bed is going to have a hysterectomy tomorrow and is not being brave about it. The room is filled with anxious relatives, hurried movement, gifts, tears, perfume. Bettina lies very still, oppressed with all the perfumes thrust up her nostrils by the women fluttering the air in that room. She has never realized before just what a self-indulgent habit perfume is, how intrusive on those who must inhale it without having selected it, what an imposition, she lies there imagining the women who go with the overwhelming scents, and none of the images are kind.

The night nurse finally clears the room of its visitors and quiets Mrs. Ginsberg with a strong sedative. Bettina has deposited her capsule in her Kleenex box and it seems to her that she remains awake through all of that long night, although that is not completely true. She seems to feel unusually restless. Perhaps it is the stranger who has taken Mrs. Callaghan's place, perhaps it is something in her own body, tonight she is especially aware of the nerve-irritating sensation of healing, as if her flesh is curling and twisting and drying.

It is an uneventful night on the floor; there is nothing but the peaceful murmur of the nurses at the station. Father Sebastiano does not come, and neither does Mischa. Bettina moves restlessly in her bed. Will it ever be day?

She slides into a troubled sleep, dreaming that she is walking down a dark street. The headlights of a truck pass across her eyes. She sees holes of white in the night, she hears the truck approaching. With wild dream terror, she wills it past her, in an enormous effort of concentration she lifts it up and moves it past her, it goes safely around her, she is spared

and then, while she is savoring the miracle of her escape, she hears the motor again, the truck has turned and is following her, creeping like an evil slithering beast after her

and she begins to run, with all of her strength she tries to run, but suddenly her feet are heavy, it is as if enormous weights have been tied to her legs, she cannot lift them, they barely come off the ground, they sink down into the surface of the road, which has become thick and sticky

and the truck is coming after her, she feels it strike her, go over the top of her like a steam roller, the highway is smoothly surfaced with her black blood. . . .

She comes awake instantly, shaking. Immediately, she knows where she is, she feels again her constant level of discomfort, remembers her accident, her condition, recognizes that she has been dreaming. Mrs. Ginsberg, heavily sedated, has not stirred at the sound of her half-scream, but continues to breathe heavily through her mouth.

Bettina is alone, panting slightly with fright, terrified that she will drift into sleep again, back into that nightmare. She manipulates her mind, stuffing it with something else, with

Piero, with Piero, she makes herself remember the excitement of his body, his soft soft lips

It was almost day; there was just barely enough light for her to see the vague shapes of the nondescript furniture in the dorm room she shared with Hoss. She came awake with a sense of arousal, a joyous wonderment, and then suddenly she was remembering . . . Piero had come back to her . . . he was here beside her, all the Christmas and birthday presents she had ever dreamed of were here, now. . . .

Without discussion, Hoss had departed for the john last night to brush her teeth, and never returned. No big deal. She'd probably bunked with one of the other girls on the floor for the night. This was a place where you had to punch the wall and yell for the couple in the next room who were shrieking and jostling to do it more quietly. . . .

Daylight was softening, illuminating,

clarifying. Bettina propped her head up with her hand and watched Piero sleep. He lay on his side, facing her, almost completely uncovered, only one leg still remained entangled in the sheets.

She examined him with wonderment, his muscled chest with its delicate nipples, the tiny golden hairs coming up his exposed leg, the smooth arm reaching as limply and expectantly toward her as Adam waiting for the touch of the finger of God

and he was hers. . . .

"Good morning!" says the nurse cheerfully, coming into the room. "I'm sorry to wake you, Mrs. Ginsberg, but we've got to prep you for your operation. Here, I have something to relax you a little, and make it easier for you. Don't be afraid."

Bettina lies beyond the bustle of the nurse and an orderly transferring the frightened woman to a stretcher for the trip downstairs; she is still panting slightly with the tail-end of a dream orgasm, wild with regret for having thought that she had forever.

The nurse pulls the curtain around Bettina's bed, the plastic wheels squeaking slightly as they run around the steel rod overhead. Bettina's arm is lifted, a wet cloth is passed down it. The air touching the damp skin is cold; it seems to Bettina that she is always cold, there is not heat enough in the universe to heat her.

"Beautiful day out there," the nurse is saying cheerfully. "A little bit chilly, but bright. We'd better hang on to these good days while we can." The staff coming in from the outside world always announces the news of the weather.

"It's looking good, baby, it's looking good," says Dr. Greshak, whistling between his teeth as if he's seeing something quite sexy. He's changing the dressing on Bettina's head, trying to make her lose track of the fact that he's doing it. "We'll be done here in a minute, hang on, Bettina. Good girl."

Mrs. Ginsberg is brought back from the Recovery Room still asleep. The operation is over and has been uneventful. The orderly and the nurses murmur efficiently to one another as they transfer her back into her bed, "I've got her here, a little bit more, okay, okay, one . . . two . . . three!" The woman groans slightly, and then is still. Her husband sits beside her, murmuring over and over, "It's finished and you're okay, Lena. It's finished and you're okay. . . ." There is a fresh scent of flowers in the room.

Bettina wakes from a sleep in which she has been dreaming of eating fruit, and remembers Mischa's apple that she has been savoring for a couple of days. She reaches her hand along the top of the night-table for it, knocking the apple down. It hits the floor with a sound like a blow to the head. Bettina hears the scramble of Mrs. Ginsberg's husband crawling under the bed, he pants and mutters, retrieving it, and she clenches her teeth, knowing she shouldn't have tried to get that apple by herself, she should have asked, but she didn't want to do that, she isn't going to accommodate the darkness, ever. Her mother puts the apple in her hand. She sets it on her chest, cupping her hand around it like a beloved little doll.

The room is crowded with visitors for Mrs. Ginsberg. They have brought jars that they open up to spoon herring on crackers, cheese spread, they are passing around treats to one another, having a feast. The nurse comes in, telling them, "I'm sorry, but some of you will have to leave, the patient is only permitted two visitors at a time." Some of the visitors leave, making an obvious exit. Within minutes they are back, they have come up the fire stairs and slipped in while the nurse isn't looking.

Bettina's mother decides to feed her Mischa's apple. With the bruise in it, it won't survive anyway. Besides, the girl has been nauseous all day and hasn't been eating, and her mother thinks to tempt her with slivers of fruit cut with Greg's penknife. The flavor of the apple reminds Bettina of a hundred images of home, she is thinking again of when she was a child.

"Another mouthful?" her mother asks her, and slides a second piece of apple into her mouth.

It is almost more than her uneasy stomach can take. She lies still for a long time after swallowing it, trying to forget that she has, and concentrates on listening to her mother playing *briscola* with Greg on the covers of her bed. After all the visitors finally leave, the taste of the apple lingers on Bettina's tongue, souring up more and more as she drowses.

She finds herself growing increasingly nauseous. She does not want to vomit, God, she never wants to vomit again, she lies so quietly she could fool ghosts into thinking she is asleep, so that she will not have to vomit.

Something is wrong.

She is floating in trembling pain, tremendously cold, she is feeling sick, feeling sick, willing herself to sleep so that she can forget it, but she is haunted with dreams of waking up too sick for school.

In the bed next to hers, Mrs. Ginsberg is throwing up, probably some forbidden food coaxed into her by her family. "Dammit, I'm too sick to be sick," she's saying angrily, not intending to be funny. The nurse changes her bed, and calls downstairs for Mischa to clean up the floor.

By the time he arrives with his pail, Mrs. Ginsberg has been cared for, and, stomach empty, is sleeping peacefully. Bettina listens to the water dripping as Mischa wrings his mop. The air is sharp with the scent of disinfectant. She receives the sensation of sound and smell through a diaphanous curtain of exquisite sickness, delicate drops of sweat have sprung up all over her face, she is shaking with that infinite cold.

"Mischa . . ." she whispers carefully. God, if she vomits now, surely her gut will come up, she is tearing loose inside. Has he heard her? It seems to her she can still distinguish the slight wash of his mop through the pounding sound of her own heartbeat, through the violent movement of the earth on which her bed stands, she dares not move, she dares not inhale all the way.

"Please . . . Mischa . . ."

"Yes, miss?"

He has heard her. Thank God, thank God, she has made contact.

"Please . . . please, help me. . . ." She manages to articulate that much, swallowing down her escaping soul, and then has to stop. She hears him run. She lies trembling, her mouth and eyes closed, as if by not opening any holes she can hold everything in. *Hurry, Mischa, hurry, damn you.* . . . The nurse is there almost immediately, but Bettina feels a rising hysteria, she cannot hold herself together, her legs will crack apart and she will flow out. . . .

The nurse takes her pulse, her blood pressure, and says something to Mischa. Bettina hears the beginning of it; she has fainted before the end.

She comes to briefly on the stretcher taking her running to the operating table to close up the rupture on her kidney. No, she is Jennifer, and they are taking her away to die. . . . She hears Mischa's voice, and knows she is holding on to his hand, she begs him desperately, "Please, don't let go . . . please. . . ."

and the orderly, running alongside the stretcher, squeezes her hand so hard she can distinguish the pain through her distress, and he answers her, over and over, "I am here, I am here...."

and then it seems to her she can hear Piero's voice, far away, he is crying out to her frantically, *Bettina, non puoi morire, non puoi morire . . . Bettina. . . .*

but she knows, it is possible to die
and suddenly she is afraid
for she doesn't want to die.

She goes down a very small hole, screaming to the orderly, "Don't let go . . . don't let go...." but she cannot hear if his voice is answering her.

They are covering her with pink roses. They are closing her into a beautiful box lined with harsh cheap satin. Step by step they are following the ritual of wiping her out of existence, carrying her to the hole in the earth

and the effeminate voice is saying peevishly, "The funeral must be styled!"

No . . . please, no. . . .

The weight of the earth comes down on her, crushing her, the top of the casket is collapsing under a depth of dirt as tall as a man, it flattens her bones, there are splinters and rotted cloth in her mouth, she cannot breathe *but I'm not supposed to be breathing*

she fights the stifling, she is wild to breathe....

"See, your father's at peace, now." She touches his face, and it is green with putrefaction, her hand falls through it

and it is her face.

"Bettina! Bettina!"

They are holding on to her. She can feel their hands. She moves her lips. *Don't let go* . . . but there is no sound

oh God oh God oh God

she falls into God and He isn't the delicate old God the Father she has been fancifying, He is an infinity of obscurity, without form, a hooded figure with no face

she cannot remember the reason for her dying, she cannot remember an old age, an illness. She is haunted with half-memory, a Kleenex box with medium-hard yellow capsules, yellow capsules in aromatic black tobacco, Kleenex box, two glasses of water, she has been hoarding her own death but cannot remember the accomplishing of it, regretting success.

She stands in a horse-drawn carriage with her arms lifted into sunlight warm as water,

crying out, "I never want to be dead...."
never wanting to be dead.

Piero's voice is everywhere, "Bettina, Bettina, Bettina..." so far away, five thousand miles away, "Bettina...Bettina...Bettina..."

She is losing him
screaming soundlessly, *Piero...Piero... I'm here....*
but he does not hear her.

She is sliding and slipping and shifting in an endless confusion, not knowing who she is, what she is.
Bettina...I am...Bettina....
and a voice answers her, "Bettina!" breaking through, and it is Mischa, the orderly.

She goes up and down the hole a hundred times. *Damn you, Dr. Greshak....* He is sending her into deep sedation, he is hiding her from her mind until he is finished with her body
not knowing that she almost escapes him.

The window is open, she can tell that. She

can smell fresh air, and it seems she can hear a bird, not a singing bird, but a cheeper, a scrounger. Sunlight is coming through the thin blanket on her leg, she can feel the warmth of it.

There are voices talking, Greg, Mischa. Once it seems to be Father Sebastiano. "Definitely a better line," he says, clearly.

She scampers within her body, teased by the thought. Football? hockey? architecture? titillated by her small race in the holocaust that is her body. She can feel the hands of women touching the enormous still shell of her; once it is the caress of a man's hand on her cheek, there is a difference in the skin on that hand, in its touch. *I'm here,* she tells the living. *I'm here.* The everlasting bird distracts her with its chirping. She wanders down the dark passageways, confused, after that noisy bird, wandering, lost. . . .

The sunlight moves slowly up the length of her leg, she goes away and returns and it is still there, crawling onto her still hand like a friendly furry sloth moving with tremendous deliberateness, going across her wrist and up her arm.

She was a child, waking up to the

touch of her mother's hand on her forehead, "Why, Bettina, the fever's gone."

"Mom, could I please have an orange."

and she lay listening to the sound of her mother in the kitchen, cutting the orange on the bread board, she was already imagining the sweet sharp juice on her tongue, she was swallowing saliva, exultant, *I'm well, I'm well*, in a minute she would sit up, shaking, and put on her old bathrobe and walk, anywhere she wanted.

There is a sword in her side, a piercing sword, dead Christ on the cross probed by the Roman lance, Don Rodrigo dying in the plague of Milan, her mind is imprinted with death, but the pain persists, increasing, a wonderment, a confusion: *death should not hurt so much...* and she begins to remember
the run to the operating room, the old tear in her kidney that had begun to heal had come apart again, the doctor with the hands that smell of cigarettes has held her kidney again,

What's his name, what's his name. . . .

Her mother is kissing her. Bettina can smell her mother's perfume, she can hear her mother's voice saying to someone else in the room, "I'm going down to the coffee shop, do you want me to bring anything back?"

The coffee shop. Images too ordinary for heaven and hell fill the soft darkness in Bettina's head: the brown scent of coffee, the invisible grease specks of hamburgers, hanging in the air, middle-aged comfortably moneyed volunteers in pink uniforms and costly white duty shoes struggling with orders, candy bars in metallic wrappers next to the cash register, neat racks of potato chips in bright cellophane. . . .

and she begins to comprehend the small familiarities that are claiming her, she must still be of the flesh, for an immortal soul does not recognize the existence of a potato chip.

"Is she smiling?"

"Mischa . . ."

"Yes, Bettina. Yes. I am here."

She raises her hand, feeling the movement of the tube hooked into her arm, there is the small rattle of the tools of her salvation. A human hand takes hers. It has real bones in it, hard strong bones that do not crumble when she weakly grasps it. The hand closes on hers, responding.

She is engulfed in an increasing roar of pain; in a moment she will have to tell someone about it or faint

but of course fainting, too, is a function of life, the tortured souls of hell do not faint, and that is the hell of it.

The sweat on her upper lips rolls like a tear, and even that is a reassurance.

She is in a semi-private room with a woman who suffers from ulcers. Nobody ever comes to see Mrs. Berenson, a widow with a son who is a Hari Krishna. Funny thing about Kevin: he had always been so hairy, beard, long hair, the whole bit. Now he has shaven off the hair, wears the saffron robes, hands out the pamphlets of salvation, chants, has given himself to a god of strangers who is as unnatural to the red hair Kevin now denies himself as white men doing blackface. His mother has not seen him in two years while he pursues souls. She bleeds alone.

"And yet, Mrs. Berenson, is wonderful, ulcers," says Mischa. What he tells her, expressing himself with difficulty, is that although the mechanism is not running perfectly, its very faultiness emphasizes the fact that it is still running. "Do you not see? You live, Mrs. Berenson. Bettina, you live. . . ."

Bettina does not respond to him. Sometimes it seems to her that since she came back from her small death, she does not breathe without reminding herself to do it, she is hanging in a dimension without time, an existence without consequence. She has checked the drawer of her night table in this new room where she has been brought and found her hand lotion and dusting powder and Piero's letters, put there after her operation. The half-empty box of Kleenex is there, too, but the capsules are gone, discovered, disposed of.

For a moment, thought of what that must have meant to somebody, her mother, a nurse, Greg, Mischa, lingers in her mind, but without emotion, without regret; she forgets about it almost immediately, something unimportant out of her past, no longer pertinent. Her soul stands in a different place, now. She has progressed past her anger at life, to an all-enveloping indifference to the fact that she is condemned to live.

"You're different, now, Bettina," says her mother. "I don't know exactly how to describe it, but . . . different. . . ."

Some men come home from the wars exactly the men they were when they left home. Most do not. Even home is different.

Someone comes into the room. "Another letter from Italy, Bettina," says a girl's voice, a volunteer with the mail. "My, what a pretty stamp."

Bettina reaches her hand for Piero's letter. "I'll have my mother read it when she gets in," she says. The volunteer gives her the letter and moves on, fooled.

Bettina has not opened a single one of Piero's letters since the accident, they gather in a growing stack in her night table drawer, existing like a small hidden fire, roaring, she is always aware of them, terrified of them, they are a constant temptation, at any moment of the day or night she could ask someone, "Please, will you read. . . ." any passing stranger will oblige . . . but her soul is not strong enough for his love . . . his pain . . . his devastating kindness. . . .

It is now the depths of winter. The commercials on the ever-present TV talk endlessly of Christmas giving, from Santa cards to Cadillacs. Steam hisses in the old hospital pipes, smelling slightly of rusted metal. Mischa coming into the room from the outside brings cold air in the folds of his coat, brings the scent of snow.

"How do you like the United States, Mischa?" Mrs. Berenson asks him. It is a question Americans are asking him constantly.

How can he answer in his meager English? He's learning rapidly, but still it's a struggle. What he manages to tell them is that he is not by training a sailor, that was simply the instrument of his escape. He is a writer.

"What do you write, Mischa? Stories?"

"Stories? Yes, Mrs. Berenson. Stories of human soul."

"The human soul . . . my God. . . ."

"It frightens you, human soul?"

"Oh, no, no. It's just . . ."

It's just that stories to Martha Berenson mean Jacqueline Susann and Harold Robbins and a little titillation and a lot of manipulation and the human soul, after all. . . .

"Some day, Mrs. Berenson, I write very big story. Very big story of human soul."

"Wouldn't it be a laugh if the great American novel ends up being written by a Russian?" says Bettina.

"The great American novel? With

his English?"

"Some day, Mrs. Berenson. I learn English, and then I write such a story...."

It is not, however, a talent he can convert immediately into food and bed, which is why he is here at the hospital. After all, he arrived in the States with just the flesh on his bones, the rough sailor's clothing of summer he was wearing at the time of his defection, and an old guitar on his back.

From the little he tells them, Bettina extrapolates the whole of his experience: Mikhail Antonych arriving into this life at the hospital is as unfamiliar with the world of the attendants and orderlies he finds here, the Jamaicans, blacks, Puerto Ricans, as a Martian stepping out of a space ship. He shares with his fellow workers the difficulties of the job, the ugly numbing hours of work, pushing patients in wheelchairs and on stretchers, mopping up vomit, cleaning, carrying, they are hands, they are backs. He shares nothing else.

Some of the people working with him are conscientious, some are not. Some are his good friends, some resent him. Many of them do not speak English or any language with which he is familiar. Most of those who do speak English do it in a manner completely outside the training he had in school, it is like having a frame hung lopsided on a picture: The center is all right, but there are empty spaces, there are spaces left over. Some of the other men have the dreams of the young, wanting to tool past the local high school in a flashy sports car, horn honking. Others are trapped by the desires of poverty, possession, to own, a great many brightly colored clothes, shoes falling out of the closet, colored TVs.

"Do you miss Russia?"

Mischa doesn't answer right away. Finally he says, slowly, "Sweetest air in the world is in Leningrad. . . ."

It is not the answer Mrs. Berenson was asking for.

Bettina can tell when Mischa is coming down the hall. "Mischa . . . Mischa . . ." the female voices murmur, aides, volunteers, nurses. There is an expanding swirl of sound, small laughter, a hundred little things that distract him from his path to Bettina's room. For always, ultimately, he heads for her.

In the first days after his defection, in the Siberia of his soul, he came simply to sit with her, not asking anything of her except that he not be alone. Sometimes she'd hear him whispering to her in Russian; she never distracted him by asking him what he was saying when he did that, she allowed him the illusion that when he stopped speaking, she would answer him in his language. It still happens occasionally that she wakes up in the middle of the night and finds him sitting silently with her, but his visits of desperation are becoming infrequent, he is beginning to make a life for himself.

She listens to the movement going on in the hall as he approaches her room. Eventually he will arrive, but he is pulled this way and that as he comes. Everybody knows that it is his dream to go to California. "Why California, Mischa?" "You ask man who grows up in Russian winters, why California?" The girls on the staff are constantly giving him little gifts, literature on the golden state, sunny posters to hang in his basement dungeon, they tempt him with coffee, with homemade brownies.

"Bettina, Dr. Greshak says you leave bed. You wish for me to put you in chair?"

Bettina hears him and doesn't hear him, she is languidly pursuing her own thoughts. Mischa does not let her escape. "Bettina, I move you?"

"I don't care."

"Is answer of child."

He's right. Children shrug and look out of

expressionless faces and say "I don't care" because that is protection. She can feel Mischa trying to lift her from her bed. She is passive, letting him do it, she is an enormous boulder dropped by the glacier passing through the Hudson Valley, she is an oversized grandmother sitting senilely in a chair in the corner.

"Come on, Bettina, help him," says her mother, and Mrs. Berenson echoes, "Yeah, Bettina, give him a hand, he's one skinny kid, and you must weigh a ton in your plaster of paris kimono."

"Let her—how do I say—indulge?"

She knows what he is trying to make her do and won't react to him. *It isn't defiance, it's nonresponse.* Even as she thinks that, she knows that she is making a decision to nonrespond. Mischa has done that to her. In spite of herself, he isn't allowing her the luxury of simply drifting. After a moment he lifts her anyway, breath jerking out of him with the effort. She's not going to help him, *damn you.* . . . She can feel the straining of the muscles of his arms, they seem to be contracting into pure stone. There is sudden sweat against her forehead from his neck.

She had fallen asleep in front of the

TV. Since her tonsillectomy, she had been afraid to fall asleep in bed, and her parents had been letting her drowse off anywhere she wanted, on the chair, on the floor, anywhere. Most of the time she didn't even realize when they took her to bed; she would waken in the morning in her room filled with sunlight and familiar toys, and she could get up and run away and so she was not afraid, but climbing into bed at night was black and terrifying, the light would be put out as soon as she wasn't watching, and so she would lie awake, so that it wouldn't be.

This time she was wakened, part way, as her father carried her up the stairs. She held on to his shoulders with both her hands, but tenderly, knowing he would not drop her, it was a love clutch

and he was singing her a song, "The Wacs and the Waves are winning the war, parlay-voo, the Wacs and the Waves are winning the war, parlay-voo . . ."

*   *   *

Mischa puts her down in the chair by the window, propping the heavy leg in the cast so that she will be more comfortable. But she does not want to be Bettina-in-a-chair-in-the-hospital.

"The Wacs and the Waves are winning the war..."

"How can you expect her to sleep, Barry," her mother asked, following them up the stairs, but they went on yelling, "Then what in the hell are we fighting for, hinky dinky parlay-voo..."

Bettina screamed the familiar words without comprehension, following her father, and her mother was saying, "You shouldn't be teaching the child that kind of language, Barry," but Bettina could see her mother's smile

and when the time came for Bettina

to go to sleep, her father lay on one side of her and her mother on the other, their hands clasping each other across her body, she could feel the weight of their arms on her chest, and she was not afraid to go to sleep

and it was never quite that good again for any of them afterward.

"Mom, I want you to go back home."
"What?"
"I want you to go back to Florence, to Renato, for Christmas."
She can hear the instant of silence as her mother is tempted by the thought but is organizing her resistance to it, and the girl rushes on, settling it at once. She hasn't the strength or the will to fight at length, she has to win immediately or not at all. If her mother doesn't capitulate immediately, she knows she will retreat within herself again and accept her mother's martyrdom and the days will continue and continue unchanged, world without end, amen.
Other voices help her, Greg, Dr. Greshak, Mischa. Bettina is now out of danger, and right

after Christmas she will be going to the rehabilitation center

and so Laura Weston Caligeri kisses her daughter and leaves

and Bettina sits in her chair beside the window she cannot see through and sees Milan's Malpensa Airport with Renato Caligeri standing beyond customs waiting for her mother, and perhaps . . . Piero. . . .

Piero walks the cold streets of Florence. She imagines a coat for him, a coat of camel's hair, expensive, and a soft light brown fur hat. Is there snow on the naked white statues in the Piazza delle Signorie? and are the young people shivering and clustering together on the Pontevecchio with their breath coming out of their mouths in little clouds? or has winter dispersed them, sent them back in every direction to their own countries, ended their dreams?

Then the images disappear, for they are unimportant and remote.

On the night before Christmas, the hospital is cleared of all the patients who can possibly be sent home. A neighbor comes for Mrs. Berenson. "Maybe if I bleed a little, they'll let me stay here," says Mrs. Berenson.

"Why, Martha, what a thing to say," murmurs the neighbor, uncertain whether Mrs. Berenson is kidding.

"There's nothing in that apartment of mine to make me want to be there on Christmas Day, Jessie, here at least there are some young people, there's something going on. I'm going to miss this place."

Bettina can hear Mrs. Berenson going away down the hospital hall, saying good-bye to the nurses. "You won't be all alone on Christmas, will you?" one of the young nurses asks, and suddenly realizing, the friendly neighbor says, "Why, do you want to come and spend Christmas with us, Martha? You know you're always welcome."

Mrs. Berenson murmurs something. Bettina doesn't distinguish the words, but she knows the tone, Dickens' poor relatives at the Pickwick feast trying not to be noticed so that they can remain.

Hoss goes home to Texas for the holidays, but leaves her roommate a gift. When Bettina opens the box on Christmas morning, she finds something soft and lacy inside. The delighted nurses looking in from the doorway tell her it is a transparent pink nightgown. The open hospital tent gowns Bettina has been wearing are part of a perpetual kidding routine about her: wallpaper on plaster walls, sexy like a rock covered with a tablecloth.

There is no way the pink gown will ever fit over Bettina's casts, but one of the nurses slits the gown up one side and drapes it on her. Everyone finds this humorous; Bettina can hear them laughing. She'd like to enjoy the moment, too, but Christmas under these circumstances is tearing her apart, she is thinking of how undertakers slit the clothing of the dead, resurrection day will be filled with people clutching their clothing cut for the convenience of the undertakers who buried them. . . .

When the phone rings, she knows it is Piero. Perhaps, after all, in some subliminal way, she has been waiting for his call on Christmas Day. The room is filled with his flowers, and he has sent her a magnificent small antique carved wooden Madonna. The ancient wood still smells lightly of forests, and when she passes her hand over it, it picks up the warmth of her flesh, in a moment the wood feels as warm as life.

She can hear Greg saying to Piero, "Yes, yes,

she is doing well. Do you want to talk to her?"

"No," she says. "No."

"Oh, come on, Bettina, it's Christmas Day. . . ."

"I won't talk to him."

"But why not?"

My God, why not?

If I touch the phone I will be touching him. It will be five thousand miles but still that wire running in the sky and under the sea and in the dirt will be unbroken, from him to me

and that I will feel.

"No," she says. "No," and puts her arm over her head, protecting the hammer of her ear from the clap of Piero's voice.

They were riding through the pink dawn in Piero's little white sports car, along the *autostrada* from Florence. They drove too fast, roaring down the cool wind, titillated, excited, with the unspoken acceptance of children in the fantasy of dying together, they were protected by their ignorance of pain.

Her hair flew in rising black strands high over her head, into his mouth, around his wrist at the wheel, she was a cloud of magic whirling around him. They were rushing to Siena, high on the mountain in the distance, Siena, city of the Middle Ages, home of Catherine, like Francis one of the mountain saints, born halfway up to God.

Siena was crowded with tourists, with young men in Renaissance costumes walking the streets carrying flags, beating drums. Checkered banners hung at the windows of the old buildings. The bell at the top of the Mangia Tower in the square tolled, for today was the running of the Palio, and old truck horses released from their shafts for the day to compete in the great race were being taken down the central aisle of the churches of their *contrade* to be blessed.

With the help of some Sienese friends, Piero obtained space for himself and Bettina at the front of the spectator section of the square around which the race would be run. The press of human bodies was so overwhelming that Bettina's hair became entangled with the buttons of the jacket of the man next to her. He tore at it angrily, muttering unfamiliar words that blackened the Italian in her soul. She could feel the pain of her torn hair, her anger at the foolish impatience of the stranger, the stumbling ruthlessness of the people pushing her in all directions, but most of all she felt the protective envelopment of Piero's arms, separating her from everyone else, clutching her to him so strongly that there was nothing between them, they were merged in a love embrace.

They witnessed parade and pageant, the twirling of the flags into the blue sky, the exhibition of the prize that would be awarded to the winning section of the city—a painting of the Madonna, the Palio after which the race was named. And finally, there was the race itself, the clatter of the horses' hooves on the pavement, the thrashing of the riders on the saddleless animals, the screams of the crowd, the mass of flesh moving like a single irresistible force carrying everything before it like the movement of the ocean, and after the race was over, the succeeding joy and disappointment, young men carried on the shoulders of their friends, small fistfights.

Afterwards Piero and Bettina went to the house of his friends to eat outside under the stars at a banquet table lit by candles and covered with delicacies the women had been cooking and storing for weeks. It struck Bettina as she looked at the tremendous lineup of fancy dishes of food, what an incredible usage of human time had gone into the preparation of this one night's eating, the shopping and paring of vegetables and chopping and frying and beating and baking and tasting and worrying

finally to be set on a washed embroidered cloth stitched by hand with ten thousand small stitches that nobody looked at, dish by dish by dish, all of it, all of it just to fill two fistfuls of space in each man's belly, and drowned in red and white wine and dropped into the dirt of the courtyard, vomited from excess, left behind and forgotten after less than one hour's space of time

and she was dismayed, aware of the tired women serving them, their hair pulled back from their pale faces, their hands curled from being in water too much, but still she was attracted by the small temptations, a spoonful of this, a nibble of that, she too was perpetuating the trivial fraud of food, entangled by her tastebuds in the inadequate employment of souls.

When finally Piero carried her away to the alley where he had deserted his little sports car, she had eaten too much, drunk too much, she felt the night wind on her face, she swallowed darkness

and woke up with her face on his lap, as he drove alongside the Arno.

"Why wouldn't you talk to him, Bets?" Greg is asking her.

"It's not the right time."

"And when will it be the right time?"

She doesn't answer him. It takes strength to lie.

"Why can't he come now, Bettina? Do you really know why you're keeping him from coming now?"

How can she tell him that Piero is part of a magic world where she is whole, he does not exist in this ugly strange metal plaster morphine world, he is in the beautiful garden at which she peeks through the keyhole without being able to reach the key and without a magic cookie to eat

and if he becomes a part of this hellish life, here, now, all she will have left

is reality.

How infinitely long Christmas Day can be, bums sitting alone on cold stone steps, GIs in World War II listening to "I'll Be Home For Christmas" on their field radios, cold stars shrivelled up in the winter sky, children peeking through the screen at a streetlight and seeing the sudden shape of a cross in the metal netting.

Christmas in a hospital, halls haunted by the sound of the patients' radios, the thin cut of pain, vomit, death. How terrible, to die on Christmas Day.

The few nurses who remain on duty have been tolerant with the visitors. It is a day that takes forever to end, with relief, for the overtaxed patients and overworked staff. The last straggling good will is finally out of the door. Only the imprisoned and the imprisoners remain, bedtime medications go slowly from room to room dispensing sleep, terminating Christmas, lights out.

Mischa comes to Bettina very late. "Where have you been?" she asks him. "I thought you had forgotten me."

"I spend Christmas being Christian." He has been covering for other men who have families. She feels the bed trembling with his fatigue as he sits beside her and leans on it.

She can guess at the unspeakable things he has done today and cries out, "Oh, Mischa, why don't you leave this hell? You don't have to stay here like the rest of us, you're free." With all the despair of her incommutable sentence, she wants him to leave, she tempts him breathlessly, "Why don't you go on to California? What are you waiting for? You can sit with your feet in the ocean and write. . . ."

"Not yet," he says softly. "Not yet."

She understands his need for the cage. Today

Dr. Greshak removed the greater part of her head bandage, giving her what he thought was a gift, the beginning of her escape from the plaster casket. In reality, what he has done is take down one of the walls protecting her. What he has done is reveal her ugliness.

It was the day of her high school senior prom. She was going with a boy who worked at her lab table in advanced biology. She was aware that today was prom day, but it wasn't something that obsessed her thoughts; she looked at the other girls in her classes who were completely occupied with expectation, and wondered, *Am I a girl?*

She worked that afternoon as she did after school every day at Willard's Pancake House. The other waitresses were women with families, raised in a different era, in a different environment. They said to her, "You should be home with your hair in curlers, honey." She had twisted a rubber band around her long hair to keep it within the regulations of the Board of Health. Early in the afternoon a customer had bumped into her while she was carrying a tray of cokes, and she was sticky. She sweated. Another waitress called in because she had a dead battery in her car, and Bettina promised to stay until the woman could get to work on the bus. One of the other waitresses offered to do it, but Bettina insisted. "I need the money," she said, but it was a bit of bravado, of disdain. "By the time you get home you're going to have twenty minutes to get dressed," said the cook. "So what?" said Bettina. "Twenty minutes are more than enough time. I can do it in ten."

She was under the shower when Brian arrived. She came to the head of the stairs in her beat-up blue bathrobe and a towel around her head to talk to him. He was wearing a rented pink tuxedo with a ruffled shirt, and looked flustered.

"God," she told him. "Whose idea was that?"

*   *   *

"A bunch of us went together to rent them."

"He has the build for it," said Mrs. Weston quickly. Thank God for mothers.

Mrs. Weston had made Bettina a soft yellow dress with a wide light green velvet belt and a bow at the back. The bow looked very young to Bettina and she took it off but then reluctantly put it back on. Her mother would surely notice. Her hair was still quite wet. She towel-dried it, saying to Brian as she walked past him into the kitchen, "Would you like a bagel? We were so busy today at Willard's that I didn't get a chance to eat."

He took the bagel smeared with cream cheese she handed him, but seemed to have forgotten how to eat in that splendiferous pink outfit of his. Bettina stood in the middle of the living room in her long yellow gown eating her bagel and combdrying her hair. Her hair was fine and straight, almost Oriental hair, reaching halfway down her hips. She did not look at herself as she combed it. It was almost a fetish with her, not to look in the mirror, the carelessness of surety.

"Oh, the hell with it," she said. "Come on, it'll finish drying on the way there." She thrust the last bit of bagel into her mouth and then pushed her hair back from her face with both hands, the girl with the long black hair, Bettina Weston.

"You look pretty," said Brian. It seemed startled out of him. She was not especially pleased to hear him say it; they had such a decent relationship, so uncomplicated, there at the bio bench. Of course she was better at bio than he was and that seemed traditionally to bother him, but they were definitely friends. Now maybe she'd have trouble with him on the way home, he might even feel he had to do something to prove his sexiness, and that was saddening, she preferred his friendship.

* * *

They had a moment of confusion at the door, uncertain who should go out first, he to hold the door open, or she to fulfill her role as a woman. They finally stumbled out together, laughing. The night air was cool on her damp scalp.

The hospital loudspeaker is calling discreetly, urgently, the signal for the heart team to go to room 381, stat, and an instant later there is the sound of the equipment being rushed down the hall to room 381, the familiar roll of rubber on linoleum, the subdued efficient exchange of necessary conversation as it passes Bettina's door.

Bettina runs her uninjured hand over the exposed portion of her head, feeling it with her fingertips. She had not known when she had two hands to use that she is so left-handed, what a follower her right hand is; making it work is exaggerated awkward movement, wooden unhandedness, a baby learning to control its new muscles.

She can feel the shape of her skull under the soft new stubble of her hair as she probes carefully around the dreadful patch of bandage, around the hole as big as Grand Central Station, she runs her hand around and around the smooth grub skull, fascinated by her nakedness.

There is the soft sound of feet running rapidly down the hall. "Father Sebastiano?" No one answers her. The footsteps go past the door, turn in the direction of Room 381, disappear.

Dear sweet Jesus. How temporary, how insecure, is the loan of the flesh. At its best, parts soon gray and fall out, parts wrinkle and weaken, or on someone's whim a human being can be sent to the Gulag and know he will not live because it is wintertime and someone has stolen his warm boots. In an instant, one can be rolled into the metal of a car, and what is the importance of beauty then?

She has an instant of acceptance, of clear wisdom in the abstract where all is possible, but the brain sits in a human skull, made of bone. *You are unfair,* she howls at that elusive God hiding beyond the end of the universe, thinking to escape her. People who are born attractive have it so much easier than those who are born ugly, who are born retarded, who are born deformed. Right from the moment they are put in their cribs at the hospital nursery, the pretty ones have the world smiling at them and God answers her softly, patiently, from inside her grub head, *Don't you think I know?*

The priest is at the door to her room. Please, the nurses know Mischa is off duty now, but will he give them a hand, since he's here? No one specifies doing what. No one has to, there's a feeling to the air.

Father Sebastiano sits, sighing, in the chair the young orderly vacates. Bettina makes believe she is drowsing so that she won't have to talk to him. They can hear the stretcher cart starting on its slow progression down the hall from room 381. Father Sebastiano does not move, does not breathe, as the sad sound goes past the door, the cart moaning slightly with its burden, followed by the tread of Mischa's workshoes on the wax surface of the linoleum.

Oh God, to die on Christmas. . . .

The elevator doors slide open, slide closed. The machinery is in motion, telephone calls, black car arriving at the back door of the hospital in the middle of the night, prayers, flowers, tears, potato salad.

She wakens suddenly. It is dawn. Christmas and Father Sebastiano are gone.

They are moving Bettina to the Brian Denlo Rehabilitation Center. People have been stopping at the doorway all morning to say goodbye, cheerful people who believe she has something to be happy about, nurses, doctors, orderlies, everyone who has participated in this foolish triumph over death.

She knows what she should be saying, but won't. *Dammit, no. I won't say thank you for something I didn't want. I have spent my lifetime writing thank-you letters for things I didn't want.*

Greg has brought the old suitcase their mother gave him when he went away to college. The nurses are filling it with the belongings that have accumulated in the months she has been here in the hospital, impersonal belongings that mean nothing to her. *Lose them. I don't care. Everything I own is replaceable.*

They tell her it is cold outside as they wrap her up in blankets. There is a moment of confusion about how to cover her bald and bandaged head. Greg takes the knit ski cap from his own head and it is stretched over her bandage. She feels the warmth of his living scalp caught in the wool.

"Oh, look," one of the nurses says suddenly. "It's starting to snow. Bettina, it's starting to snow."

The stretcher rolls, making the expected turns, she has gone down to x-ray this way a dozen times, a hundred times, a million times, she has come and gone down these halls like breathing. Now she takes a different turn, there is a rush of air and suddenly there is nothing between her and the out-of-doors, she smells winter.

"Hurry up, get her out of the snow," someone is saying urgently, and her stretcher picks up pace, running down the ramp through tiny cold stabs hitting her exposed skin, she is lifted into the ambulance, the doors are slammed shut, and it is over, the five seconds of reality she has experienced. The vehicle stuffed with the air of disaster begins its journey, taking the body from one temple of pain to another.

Mischa and Greg squat near her, kidding with each other as they tumble somewhat with the movement of the ambulance. Mischa is coming with her to the Brian Denlo Rehab Center. Being an orderly at Brian Denlo should be a different experience from being an orderly at St. Mary's. He is restive, not quite ready for California, but needing a change. Dr. Greshak has made arrangements for him. Bettina knows the doctor thinks it will help her, having the familiar orderly in the unfamiliar place. Perhaps it will even help Mischa, having her there, he needs to hang on to something, too.

The wind is piercing as they wheel her into the Brian Denlo Center. She can feel the spaces where the stitches of Greg's cap leave little holes to her bare head. A door closes after her and she has arrived. Stage two: rehabilitation. There is no more hope of escape for her. She is the prisoner of her body.

They transfer Bettina to her new bed. She is introduced to the other patient in the room, a girl named Cathy Wallenstein.

"My God, Cathy Wallenstein," says Greg. "Whatever happened to you?"

For a telltale instant no one answers, and then the head nurse who has brought them here says briskly, "Cathy fell from an overpass over Route 1."

"Fell from an overpass? What was it, an automobile accident?"

"No, not exactly," murmurs the girl. She sounds very young.

"Cathy is coming along very nicely, now," the head nurse says. "Mr. Weston, would you like to hang your sister's things in the closet?"

"There's no need to change the conversation, Miss Trevor," says the girl. "You might as well tell them. I don't care. I jumped off the overpass. I wanted to kill myself, but I guess I didn't do a very good job of it, all I did was break my back. That's why I'm in this crazy rack, they've got to keep turning me over and over, like a pancake that never gets done...."

Greg is shifting with embarrassment, Bettina feels his hand opening and closing on her arm. Poor Greg. He's never been good at intense situations. "I'm sorry," he murmurs. "It's none of my business."

"Forget it."

There is a brief second of silence after that, and then everyone gets very busy, taking Bettina's belongings out of the suitcase, settling her into the bed, but she's thinking of Cathy Wallenstein jumping from an overpass over Route 1, with cars passing in ordered rows below, people going home or shopping or rushing to mate. Screeching tires, feet trampling brakes, as she came down like Michael descending from heaven, she crashed into macadam and thought something had ended, but something else had begun.

"What direction am I pointing in, Mischa?"

She hears him opening a window, consulting the sun. "You're facing east," the head nurse, Miss Trevor, says briskly.

East. Bettina tries to orient herself, she cannot sleep until she understands the direction of her body. She recalls beds in which she has slept during her lifetime, her toes have pointed to the hospital parking lot, to her mother's room, to the Arno

but now it seems to her that her bed is

moving, around and around
east dammit east
   yet the relentless movement goes on, quickening, there is no dawning east direction, there is no dawn, there is nothing but darkness.

Someone touches her cheek, a contact touch, a nail fastening her to reality. *Mischa.* She takes his hand and holds it against her cheek.

"You like Russian novels?" he asks her. "I think maybe I read to you Russian novel. In English, of course."

"With your grasp of the language?"

"Maybe I read some, Greg read some, nurses read some. Who knows?"

She exhales slowly, knowing a different flavor of air, less antiseptic, less frightened, less quick. "*War And Peace,*" she says. "I've always wanted to read it, but never had the time. Read me *War And Peace.*"

"Is very long. Take forever."

But they both recognize that that is just about what is available to them in this place.

They make a life at Brian Denlo, different from what they knew at St. Mary's Hospital. The patients here are not usually in danger from the 3 AM visitor. Mischa is running constantly, but there isn't the level of horror in his work that there was before, he can call to Bettina as he walks past her door with a patient, he can stay with her briefly when he takes her downstairs to therapy or to sit in the sun-room.

In the evenings he brings the book as he promised. The sound of his voice reading out loud goes weaving insidiously down the halls. Slowly, slowly, out of the rooms and passageways and places beyond the stars people come to him and his story, he is the piper calling them in, they come with sighs and whispers and grunts of effort to gather in the room. Bettina hears their breathing, their laughter, their comments. They are all caught up in the moment after supper and before sleep, they congregate about her, the faceless ones.

There is a festive feeling to the meetings of this fraternity of the wounded at the end of a day of therapy, sharing the experiences on the road back. They hand the book around to one another, taking turns reading, and afterwards comment and drink orange juice and eat cookies Mischa has stolen for them from the kitchen. Sometimes he brings in his guitar and sings to them.

One day the rehab center is enveloped in an incredible snowstorm. Even Bettina knows the storm, she is aware of a strange soundlessness to the air, as if the center has been swallowed by an enormous greedy being, and they are quietly sliding down the black gullet.

She is the only one who sees the storm in black, everyone else is blasted by the whiteness. The conversation is excited, jaunty. The patients don't want the storm to end: Let it become the worst ever recorded. It is a childlike hope in which they can indulge themselves, invulnerable in their weakness, knowing they will be provided for, food stockpiles, generators, healthy outsiders alerted. Let it snow.

The snow falling outside releases old ghosts. For the first time, Mischa talks about his childhood, about other snow, a series of child-images. He sits on a small sled pulled by his father down a path that has not yet been walked by anyone, and is afraid of the tall dark trees hunched like old men wearing tufts of fur on their coats. But there is the big man up front, his laughter drifting back and circling the boy on the sled. And afterwards they enter the winter cottage where green pine logs in the fireplace snap the scent of resin into the air. "My mother waits for us. She is beautiful woman, long blonde hair, most beautiful woman in the world. . . ." and she has baked sweet cakes for them.

But he cannot hold back the true winter images in his brain. The laughing father is gray, now, "Gray and thin . . . he wears rags . . . he suffers. . . ." perhaps he is falling at this moment into the snow of the Gulag and being dragged away dead, for all of his life Mischa will not know the exact hour it happens

and the beautiful blonde-haired mother is now grown old, her face is falling into her skull from the unending onslaught of pain, and she is alone . . . she wanted him to go, but he was selfish to do it, he has left her alone. . . .

"Hey, don't think about it, kid. No sense hurting over something you can't change, right?" That's Mr. Prima, a carpenter who fell off a roof last summer and broke both his heels. "Look, let me tell you about when *we* were kids. We had a toboggan. God, that was beautiful, the whole neighborhood on the toboggan, eight, ten kids. We'd take off down Red Hill, a bunch of maniacs, it's a miracle we wasn't all killed. Steep? It was like a trip down an elevator. My sister would scream so loud they must of heard her in the next county. And of course she was always the first to start dragging the sled back up again for another run. . . ."

The others push into the conspiracy, skiing the blue snows of Chile in August, a long-ago ice boat skims across a frozen lake in another dimension, a Depression baby remembers the joy of pulling fish out from under the ice-crusted river, food beyond imagining. The stories grow, become impossible, they roar with delight.

Cathy teaches Mischa a song in German, a language she does not understand, a language her father only half-remembers. It is a song that comes from somewhere in the dirt of the farm where her ancestors lived out their lives, a slow and haunting song sung without accompaniment by the excheerleader who is strapped to an enormous stillness, her thin little soprano wavers and catches and starts up again. Mischa follows, guitar and strong male voice, stumbling and laughing and corrected and repeating, and finally, in mid-phrase, Cathy sings no more. From her genetic memory she has passed on to this stranger the song of a land that neither of them has ever seen.

When the nurse comes finally to send everyone to bed, the patients move away reluctantly on their walkers and wheelchairs, and three-legged with canes, and for many of them, years from now, the night of the soft unending snowfall gobbling up sound will be what they remember from the days they spent at Brian Denlo, becoming whole again.

* * *

Bettina does small regulated movement with her awkward arm in its reduced cast. It seems foolish at first, the therapist has to do most of the movement for her. And yet, there's something alive within the tomb, Bettina can feel the length of her muscles stretching, her shoulder joint pivots. She lies in bed, resting, after one of her sessions, and her heart beats fast, with something more than exertion. She does not analyze it, but the sound of her heartbeat continues in her head long after her breath has calmed down.

Cathy Wallenstein has a visitor from New York City on weekends, an older woman named Ara Sherwood who brings fantastic gifts to Cathy, bottles of expensive perfume, chilled caviar, champagne, fresh flowers. Ara Sherwood's voice is filled with shadows. She is the sound of a stone dropping into water, she is a Japanese beetle glistening blue-green in the sunlight, she is the mirage image rising from black tar on a steamy summer day

and Cathy, spunky, completely unremarkable Cathy, always cries after her visits.

Natasha dances at the great hall with

Prince Andrei.

Cathy comes from a small town in New Hampshire. Her father has a farm, thirty acres of hilly grazing land for cows. There is a wet dirt road, slippery with droppings, that the cows use to reach the highway which they must cross twice a day to go from the barn to the fields and back. Sooner or later everything the Wallensteins do or think or eat or dream has to do with the cows, with their eating and drinking and milking and mating and calving and slaughter. The air is constantly pervaded with their stink, it grows into the fingernails, into the hair of the humans who live with them.

Cathy came to New York City thinking to be a model, after she won a Miss Apple Blossom contest at a local movie theater. The kids from Linville High had come in a caravan of cars to yell, "Cathy! Cathy! Cathy!" at the finals. The judge had put a red velvet robe on Cathy's shoulders, and a crown on her head. She'd never known a moment like that in her whole life; she could have died right then and it would have been all right, you know?

Her parents hadn't wanted her to leave Linville, but she couldn't come out of a moment like that and then forget it. What is there in Linville for her? Marriage to a boy who works in the local shoe factory, and five pale kids and living in a trailer set up permanently on cinderblocks in a clearing in the woods. You know what it's like to live in one of those trailers, with trees behind it so tall they must be a thousand years old, they lean over you, and when you're not looking, it's like they march a little across the clearing, coming after you. . . .

But New York City wasn't what she had thought it would be. It was more, and it was less. It was bigger and taller and brighter and sparklier and richer and infinitely more desirable. It was also dirtier and lonelier and expensiver and scarier and shabbier, and it ate you up like it was starving.

Ara Sherwood ran one of the incredible number of model agencies Cathy trudged through with the 8 × 10 glossies she'd had made of herself out of the money she'd earned home babysitting and baking bread for the passing tourists. Ara had flipped through the photographs without really stopping to look at any of them, the way all of the other women at all the other agencies had done, and Cathy had stood waiting while she did that, not quite looking at all the fantastic skinny women sitting around the office. She felt her baby fat and her cuteness in this sea of New York chic, the ineptitude of her self-applied makeup job, she was overwhelmed with her own worthlessness, she was ashamed to presume.

Miraculously, Ara did not dismiss her, as everyone else had done. Can you imagine what that meant, after the weeks and weeks of rejection, of feeling as if she were losing color in the eyes of the people looking at her, of doubting whether she even cast a shadow any more? Ara had wanted to help her. She had looked at Cathy very directly, not the kind of look she was accustomed to getting from a woman, and told her that her hands might do.

Her hands! Cathy hadn't even understood at first what Ara was talking about. But she learned. It's learn or die, in the business. In modeling, the body is chopped up for merit, live anatomical specimens. Shoulders to hang clothing from. Teeth. Legs. Eyes. Hands. Hair.

And Bettina echoes, "Hair . . ."

Ara had sent Cathy to her own photographer for sample shots. Then afterwards they'd gone out together to celebrate their new association, they'd gone to lunch in a fantastic place full of pots of hanging flowers and autographed pictures of all the biggest movie and TV stars.

That night Ara had treated Cathy to a Broadway show, with tickets so close to the stage she could really see the faces of the actors. And the next day they'd gone to Saks where Ara charged good clothes for her, clothes Cathy would never have thought of wearing by herself, but you wouldn't believe how beautiful they were, and how wonderful they made her look.

Of course Cathy was embarrassed by all this generosity, but Ara told her that she, Cathy, was the one doing the favor. Can you believe that? But Ara was a lonely woman. In the midst of all the glamor, in the constantly turbulent and frantic life, there was no real emotion, no real affection. Cathy's inexperience and excitement made everything more interesting for Ara; Ara actually made Cathy feel as if she were the one doing the giving, her acceptance was the gift.

Life was wonderful for Cathy, the working, the going out with Ara, the being beautiful, and all of it was because of her new friend. She'd have done anything for Ara. Anything.

And Ara brought her to see the apartment where she lived at the very top of a skyscraper, the large and unbelievable apartment filled with antiques and plants and a balcony that opened right out into the sky.

Foolish Natasha falls in love with love

and is betrayed

and Cathy cries.

The cast is taken from Bettina's arm. Air comes in on her flesh that is stiff and knows no sensation. There is the stench of old sweat, and the nurse bathes the skin layered with dead cells, gently rubbing the crust from the living flesh
 thin thin arm, the arm of a survivor of Dachau or Auschwitz
 and Mischa brings vodka and Fritos and patients and visitors crowd the room in celebration.

Breakfast. Therapy. Lunch. Nap. Therapy. Conversation in the sun room.
 People playing cards, "Read them and weep," and, "Lucky in love . . ."
 Dominoes clicking.
 The sound of Cathy being turned on her rack.
 Mischa's laugh somewhere down the hall.
 Time unending, measured in large denominations. Is there still a world outside Brian

Denlo where seconds matter?

Laughing cheerful visitors.

Patients going home filled with hope, with acceptance.

Winter ending, winter lost, winter never having been at all for Bettina, except for the tiny instants when she passed from door to door, St. Mary's to Brian Denlo.

Pierre climbs the hillside in excitement to observe the battle he is helping to finance, and staggers down again afterwards gasping over value received.

Ara Sherwood smells like sandalwood, like expensive lingerie, like hundred-dollar cashmere sweaters. She coaxes Cathy with petits fours, "Come on, baby, you know you always liked petits fours, I could never keep enough on hand for you," greedy little Cathy

and Cathy says petulantly, her voice unfamiliar with childishness, "I only made believe I liked them because I thought you wanted me to eat them. I always hated them. I hated them!"

Ara murmurs, "Oh, Cathy . . ." and the rack is turned.

* * *

Bettina's mother calls her from Florence. She is very busy these days entertaining for her lawyer husband; as she tells Bettina about it, she slips into speaking Italian without even realizing she's doing it. Her voice sounds bright and happy.

There is very little Bettina can say to her: "I can move my arm by myself, now. I think I'm putting on weight." The kingdom of the flesh, this place is dedicated to the flesh. It's hard to remember here that anything else matters.

Just before she hangs up, her mother tells her that Piero has been out to the Ferrari summer home in the mountains making a bedroom out of an enclosed porch that looks out over the valley. The air is very pure there, and they had all thought that perhaps when the weather is milder, perhaps when Bettina is ready to leave Brian Denlo, she could go . . .

and Bettina hangs up softly.

Cathy makes excuses for her own parents who have never called her since Bettina came to Brian Denlo. "They're not too great on the telephone," she says. "Besides, they're awful busy. People don't realize what a responsibility it is to have animals, there's never a day off, never a chance to get away. The damned cows won't stand around waiting for you."

They had visited Cathy and Ara once in their apartment in the sky. Mr. Wallenstein had fumbled with the tiny canapés and cocktail hot dogs on colored toothpicks on the low glass coffee table. Mrs. Wallenstein had dumped the caviar on her cracker into the potted rubber tree because she didn't like the taste of fish. And just as Cathy was assuring them that she was perfectly safe here in the City, a police car had gone down the street below, its siren screaming. God, but that was funny!

Bettina sits beside her bed, waiting for the nurse to take away the basin she has been using to wash her face and hands.

"What are you doing?" Cathy asks her.

"Trying to figure out what I look like now."

She is running her hands over her face, her head, her neck. She is thin; it is simple now to know the reality of the skull beneath the flesh. The cheekbones end, she feels her teeth, the muscle tying the jawbone to the skull, the slight depression formed in the developing bone by the ribbon she always wore tied around her head when she was a child. Ugly. Ugly. Ugly. Her hair is a fifties Marine butch except for the area always haunted with soft headaches where

hair will never grow again
and blank eyes stare like battered aggies nobody bothers to claim after the game is over.

Prince Andrei is dying

Cathy will not listen to the death. "Read it some other place, will you? You guys can go anyplace you want, I'm the one stuck with the damned machine."
Mischa wheels Bettina to the sun room with the book, followed by the others who have been listening in on the nightly readings, the half-people, the past-people, the halt and the lame and the blind hobbling after like the beggars before they touched the robe of Christ. They all settle somewhat self-consciously around Bettina's wheelchair to listen to Mischa's familiar, accented voice as he reads, everyone is so taken with the story that they no longer correct his mispronunciations. Afterwards they stream slowly back to Cathy's room so that she can be in on the continuation of the story. "You should have heard it, Cathy," they tell her. "It would make you understand death better." She doesn't answer them. The girl who jumped from the overpass on Route 1 doesn't want to

hear about death.

"Bettina. Please, I know how hard it is for you to get to sleep, but will you talk to me?"

"What's the matter, Cathy? Do you want me to ring for the nurse to give you something?"

That isn't the escape Cathy wants. "Could we just talk?" But she has difficulty starting. "It's that damned book of Mischa's. Can you believe it? It's unreal, crying over something that never even happened...."

Bettina lets herself down from her bed and drags herself to Cathy. They kid about the rack that holds her constantly, but this is the first time Bettina has actually touched it. The rotating bed seems to hold pain like the ghosts of Andersonville and Buchenwald, it is a medieval torture rack, a tool of the Inquisition, the bed of Procrustes.

She touches Cathy, this human being hanging face downwards staring into her own darkness. Oh God, the flesh is warm but the body is dead, and Bettina's hand is cold with tears.

"I'm not getting any better, Bettina. Do you think I'm going to die?" Weeks and months have been passing and the conversation has always been bright and hopeful, but there's no denying, nothing has changed.

"Don't get discouraged, Cathy," Bettina tells her. "These things take time. It seems to me you're eating better now...." and there are half-remembered echoes in her lie, but does the girl want the truth?

Brian Denlo is very quiet around them. There isn't a sound anywhere, everyone on the floor is asleep but them. "Go on back to bed, Bettina," Cathy says gently. "You shouldn't be up like this."

The dawn never comes. "You know why I tried to kill myself, don't you," Cathy whispers. Does she know Bettina is still awake? Perhaps she wants to be uncertain whether she is heard as she describes her father looking around the chic rooms of Ara Sherwood's apartment and asking roughly, "What's really going on with you two . . . ?"

The bus Cathy took after her parents had left was the first one she could find that was leaving Port Authority terminal, any bus to away. She sat beside a window waiting for the bus to leave, terrified that it would not be quick enough. Finally the bus started up, blasting noise and the awful stench of wasted gasoline; the leviathan moved, carrying her out of the city and under the river to Jersey.

For a little while as they travelled, she let

herself believe that she was going home, but there were no mountains on the horizon, nothing but incredibly ugly gray industry and an indefinable stink that seeped around the edges of the dirt-coated bus window, and finally she had to accept it: she would never go north again.

She got off the bus and walked to an overpass and without really thinking about it, climbed over the railing and let go.

The night is silent. Finally, sighing, Cathy settles down to sleep.

Bettina lies awake, trembling, exhausted. *Oh God, I wish I had some answers.* Why questions without answers? *Why give me a brain that's too good and not good enough. . . .*

and there is only the simple reality of the tiptoeing steps of the nurse coming down the hall to turn Cathy on her rack.

"Dr. Greshak, I want to go home."

"What have you got against Brian Denlo? It's one of the best rehab centers in the northeast."

"That's not the issue." How does she explain to this competent old man who can walk away from this place any time he wants, what it's like to be here, the breath of deformity, the hundred unclean spirits lurking in the corners?

"I'll never get my head straight in here. I need to be out of this cocoon and into the world, I've got to start living with real people, normal people. Please, let me go home." *I must escape, I've had enough. . . .*

There is a silence while he considers. Finally he asks her, "And where is home, Bettina?"

It is a lonely question that has occupied her during the dark hours after everyone else on the floor is asleep. Is Barnard home? Is her mother's and Renato's apartment in Florence? Or the room prepared for her overlooking the valley, where the air is pure? Ultimately, she has decided that right now home for her is Greg's apartment, casually kept, stinking of Miss Moss's cats, empty all day while her brother works. It is all she has left.

"And if I send you home, can I trust you, Bettina?"

"Can I trust you, Dr. Greshak?"

He's talking about the Kleenex box. She's talking about the decision he has made to wait and try her corrective surgery until she is walking. If the operation fails, will the fact that she is walking make her better able to handle a life sentence of blindness?

*   *   *

The nurse is helping Bettina to dress for her trip home. Ara Sherwood is in the room, too, visiting Cathy with a gift of fresh strawberries and whipped cream flavored with French cognac in a wide-mouthed thermos.

"I want to go home too, Ara," Cathy wheedles. "There's no reason why I have to stay in this crummy place. You can pay a nurse to take care of me at the apartment. It must cost a bundle for me to be here, it might even be cheaper for you if I'm at the apartment."

When Mischa comes to take Bettina away in the wheelchair, Cathy cries out, "We can get a derrick and hoist this whole damned contraption. . . ."

"Here, Cathy, you haven't eaten your strawberries. The whipped cream is going to go sour if you don't eat it soon."

"Ara, you're not answering me. Can't I please go home?"

"We'll have to wait and see what the doctors say," the older woman tells her finally. "For now you mustn't get excited, it's bad for you." The calm voice is a death to dreams.

"So who's excited?" Cathy's voice is high-pitched, wavering. "See, I'm calm. Okay, so I can't leave right now. But I'm going soon. Hey, Bettina, as soon as I get out of here, I want you to come and visit us, you're not going to believe how beautiful our apartment is. . . ."

Fumbling, Bettina kisses Cathy. "I'll stop by every time I come for therapy." It's time to go. To stay longer would be to punish.

"We're going to have a bash at the apartment, Bettina. You'll see. I'll walk around and show it to you, and you'll see the view."

Bettina chokes on the air of Brian Denlo. She holds her breath until Mischa pushes her chair outside into the bright fresh air.

She sits in the bedroom Greg has set aside for her in his apartment, and listens to the clock ticking. It is an old wind-up clock that used to be in the house of her childhood. "Oranges and lemons," say the bells of St. Clemens, but now the clock doesn't say that anymore, it has an odd instant of laryngitis as if it is always on the verge of clearing its throat.

The refrigerator stops vibrating in the kitchen, and she realizes just how unbearably noisy it was while it was on. But the awareness passes instantly. She sighs, overstuffed with time.

She began this morning of her first day alone in the apartment in combat with a sock. She had not realized before that moment of rock-bottom confrontation just how much she had been dependent on people at St. Mary's Hospital and at Brian Denlo, she had never had a moment alone, she had even longed to be lonely. . . .

Whoever had washed her sock had left the top partially folded inwards so that to her fumbling fingers it seemed that there was a toe at either end, and no hole for her foot to enter. *This is stupid,* she'd told herself, trying to make it all into nothing, but there was desperation in her gut, tears, hysteria. Yesterday she could have held it up and someone would have solved the problem for her, Cathy, a passing nurse, somebody, second-hand eyesight.

She knew now that she had been cheating ever since she was blinded, she now had to really live with it. Finally, randomly, her fingers discovered the inward curl of the cuff and she put on the sock, almost an anticlimax. She told herself she had done it alone, some kind of a victory, and it should have made her feel good, but she was strangely disconsolate.

Beyond the bedroom window open to tentative spring there are birds, their voices different from the lonely birds of winter. Their voices are briefly beautiful with the temptations and necessities of spring. She hears the hum of a small airplane on its way to someplace, and there's a dog barking somewhere, not warning, not angry, just barking and barking, the always present barking dog.

She sits there listening and remembering the look of Miss Moss's back yard, the ancient ivy, the tremendous shadows under the big old trees, the dampness, rough bark green with moss and rot, green, everything green. If she had never seen at all she would not know green, and she wonders what the always-blind see in their heads when people speak of green, is it after all another shade of black? But ultimately it is a small consolation, the having seen, for you cannot feel the loss, when you have never seen at all.

She pulls herself to a standing position. Now that the cast on her leg is diminished, she can even move for a short distance with the help of crutches, but the weight of the plaster is still considerable, and she has to be careful of the wounded kidney. She stands at Miss Moss's large old-fashioned window, leaning her palms on the sill, thrusting her head out into the dear warmth of sunlight, and perhaps it is that small movement of leaning forward into unseen space that is her undoing.

Imperceptibly she feels something, nothing reasoned or developing, just there suddenly, a frantic and unreasoning burst-out of fear.

Nothing has changed; she still leans with her palms on the sill, still accepts the sensation of the sun on her poor head, but she becomes aware of her desperate heartbeat, loud, swift, her heart thrashes hysterically as a wild bird new-caught in a cage.

Oh God, what's happening?

The sounds of the day are the same, the clock still *ick-a*'s, the cars still come and go on the highway in front of the house, but suddenly she is terrified.

She must throw herself out of this window. She knows a quick foretaste of how wonderful it will be when she does it, she should not hesitate, go go go, nothing to do with logic or hope or thought or anything she has ever known before, a compulsion, a phobia, go go go, and get it over with.

In another portion of her mind she frantically tries to reason, *I must move back, I must get away from the window....*

but the overriding part of her, the instinctive, the primeval, the deepest, the undeniable, is overwhelming her. She fights, screaming in her soul, trying to fill her consciousness with something else, anything to block out the compulsion, the irresistible, the siren song, the maniac

she claws up faces ... her mother's ...

Greg's . . . Piero's . . .

Help me, Piero, oh God, help me. . . .

she tears the clothing off him piece by piece, forcing lust upon herself, driving her fingernails into his golden breasts

but she is losing him, has lost him

her fingernails are into the old sill, she can feel the peeling paint pushing up under her nails

her arms shake with the desperation of holding on, her weak left arm collapses and she is tipping, she is tipping

too frightened to remember God

losing the battle with this irrational force that has nothing to do with her brief past love affair with death, it is nothing of her conscious, separate from her, a black horseman riding out of hell after her. . . .

Her distracted brain has registered the sound of the doorbell downstairs, and she concentrates frantically on that . . . *please God let it be somebody for me please God. . . .*

The sweat has broken out on her face, in her armpits, her fingers are sliding on the sill. It seems to her that she can hear the sound of Miss Moss's heavy slippers going down the hall, and the rising and falling murmur of voices

Help me please whoever you are help me. . . .

Someone is coming up the stairs to Greg's

apartment, but how slowly, how slowly, he never makes the top of the stairs, an abstract philosophical puzzle, you can never reach the door because to do that you must travel half the distance, and half of that, and half of

oh God what does it matter, what does it matter, whole lifetimes given to playing academic games with ideas that don't matter

she holds on, holds on, making herself breathe in small gasps while she waits, without distending or collapsing her chest, *Please hurry, I don't know if I can wait any longer* she is being coldly careful about not changing anything, but she cannot tell where she is any more, is she erect or leaning or falling or dead, she is frozen in a moment without time, a fly caught in fossilized amber.

How long Mischa has been holding her, she isn't quite sure. When he first came into the room, she couldn't speak, and for an instant she was afraid he wouldn't understand that she was in trouble, he would stand socializing and she wouldn't be able to do anything but succumb, fall out of the window right in front of him, bring the fragilely mended body down to solid earth below and end it. Perhaps that even began to happen, she doesn't remember.

She is confused, numb, not crying, not knowing fear any more, just shaking quietly with enormous heat in her head, although afterwards Mischa will tell her it was her paleness that alerted him to her distress.

It doesn't matter any more. She is away from the window, and Mischa is holding her and whispering. She realizes she is putting her fingernails into his flesh and wants to pull her hands away. He submits to her need and it must cause him pain, but for a stutter of time she must do it

and it is in that moment that she reaches the bottom of her descent. Not in the dark hours on the operating table. Not in the frantic days when she was hoarding up the death-capsules. Not the thief coming at three in the morning to steal her away sometime when Father Sebastiano was not watching. Now, in the quiet moments after her arm cast is gone, and there is a beginning of a new life.

She holds on to Mischa, knowing the warmth of his body, his breath, his heartbeat. She almost does not understand who it is, so close to her, she only knows without reasoning that it is a brother human being, and that is enough.

"Are you hungry?" Mischa asks her.

The ordinariness of the question is better than a flight of logic to bring her stability. He is describing what he has brought for them to eat for lunch, sliced ham, potato salad, root beer. Listening to him, she feels a sudden and overwhelming hunger; she almost cannot wait the moments it takes for him to open bundles and put food on her plate, she gulps and tears and finally puts her head down on her arms, nauseous with overeating and excitement, trembling. What has happened to her? Will she ever understand herself again?

And it comes to her, slowly, slowly: *Walls, floors, ceilings*. You have to have them, to stay alive. Without the limits, there are too many dimensions in which to fly apart, to go insane.

She has always fought against restricting rules, manners, appearances, white lies when truth does not help, religion, dress, people, a hundred thousand years of accumulation of rules

and some of them are foolish, and some of them are destroyers, but many of them are necessary for survival, even some of the foolish ones, and she who is beginning to live once more must put the floor and ceiling and walls about herself again.

She is sitting on the hood of Mischa's 1957 Studebaker at the edge of a swamp. Last night she said, "I think I can hear peepers." Greg told her she was crazy, it was miles and miles to any kind of a swamp. Maybe she was hearing a primitive beat in her own blood because it was spring. But she wouldn't be placated with fantasies, she knew she could hear the peepers, and so today Mischa has brought her to the Jersey swamplands and she is listening to spring.

Her soul is very simple, now. It is as if all the convolutions that were formerly there have been wiped out by pain, by confrontation with life-death values. There is nothing left but quietude. She almost does not want to talk any more; she knows that makes Greg unhappy, and so she forces herself to continue in conversation with him, but what she says is meaningless, gesture only, and he must need reassurance very badly to accept it.

The sunshine showering down on her is warm without discomfort. She rolls up the sleeves of her blouse to receive it, rubbing her good hand down the length of her thin slow left arm, feeling the penetration of warmth into her cold flesh working through to the glacier bones. Heat is collecting in the hood on which she sits, she can feel it through the half-jeans she wears around her cast. There is no stranger here to see her with her short hair, her pinned-together clothing, there is only her friend Mischa; the rest of the species of man exists only in the distant sounds of traffic, too far away for pain.

She hears a small splashing sound in the swamp and imagines a turtle swimming with foolish feet in the murky water, or an aquatic bird plummeting down into the reeds, or big irregular bubbles of swamp gas oozing up to the liberating air. She is sweating in her scrubby scalp, she rubs her fingertips into the short hair, feeling the wind being gobbled up by the moisture.

Mischa is bringing her silent gifts of reeds and grasses and cattails, exploded cattails soft as fairy's hair floating in the wind, and sharp little seeds, harsh biting tough little seeds, straight as soldiers on the stem, and cutting bending leaves that open cold thin lines on her fingers. It is another world continuing all the time with no man watching it, another level where creatures come and go in and out of the water, fly the sky, sun themselves, where last year's rushes make a sound like pain as they rub together. Insects land on her skin, for she is so still they do not recognize her as the enemy, she is stone, she is dropped dead tree, she is yesterday's boot left rotting in the muck.

She smells everything, damp, rotting, dusting, evaporating, in this strange, lifestuffed place. She hears voices whispering, rasping, shrilling, rubbing. Her exploded soul is so empty she contains everything.

How good it is, after all, to be alive . . . and for a moment she almost remembers such a thought, but will not let herself,

for she is beginning now.

Mischa carries her up the stairs to Greg's apartment after taking her to Brian Denlo for therapy. He is in one of his wildly cheerful moods, telling her a Russian political story about a farmer with an illegal goat, and a stuffy bureaucrat, taking all the voices, the farmer pretending to be stupid, the bureaucrat pulling rank, the philosophical goat which knows it will be eaten, it is just a matter of which set of human teeth will do it.

The cast makes her heavy and unwieldy, and she can feel the quick gasping of Mischa's breath, the wild run of his heartbeat. More than that, she knows this frantic gaiety of his, which is the way he acts when his suffering catches up to him, in an instant he will snap the tether and lose control, he will scream.

"Mischa, why are you waiting to go to California?" she asks him. "You're trapped here. You aren't happy. . . ."

He loses his balance and they tumble into the wall, her cast making a tremendous sound as it hits the plaster and the moldering cloth wallpaper printed in blue roses and dull golden stripes. They slide down three steps together and stop, sitting in the middle of the staircase, panting.

The strange hall of Miss Moss's old house is hovering with mildew ghosts; the sound of the fall has not echoed, the walls have eaten it up. But Bettina and Mischa have not escaped. Miss Moss's Eleanor Roosevelt voice calls from somewhere, "Are you all right, my dears?"

"Now you've done it," says Mischa. Is he laughing? Angry?

"Mischa? Bettina?" The thin old woman is coming down the hall, stumbling on the small pieces of rug covering the bare spots on her ancient carpet.

"Is nothing, Miss Moss. Come, join us, we make pot of Russian tea."

"Only if you let me bring the cake."

By now even Mischa is familiar with her stale crumb buns, but he answers her gallantly, "Fine. We wait for you."

"I won't be a minute. . . ." and her voice fades as she runs, this thin and transparent woman who has told them she was once betrothed to one of the richest men in the world, the heir to railroad millions. However, his mother didn't like her, and sent him on a round-the-world cruise on the family yacht to make him forget her, but he fell overboard in the China Sea during a storm and so the mother didn't get to keep him. And could that be the truth?

Or is the truth that she took care of an ailing mother, rejecting all suitors, until she was too old for marriage? Or that she is waiting for the inheritance of an uncle who refuses to die? Any or all or none, only God knows the truth, Miss Moss has probably forgotten it by now.

Mischa hoists Bettina onto his shoulder and carries her the rest of the stairs into Greg's apartment, where he deposits her into an armchair. Then he goes into the kitchen and she hears him running water into the kettle.

"Mischa . . ."

He doesn't hear her at first, she has to repeat it: "Mischa!"

"Yes?"

"You're not staying here because of me, are you? I can manage. You don't have to wait to go to California, I'll be okay."

She hears him come to the doorway of the room. After a moment he says, "You not know end of story yet. Would you believe, goat commits suicide?"

"No."

"Has heart attack?"

"Why don't we have it be a pregnant goat and the sight of the possibilities inspires the two men to greed, better a live goat producing kids than a mutton chop?"

He laughs. It seems to her to be an everyday laugh, his demons have passed. "Capitalist romantic," he says. He goes back into the kitchen, and she hears him assembling the china for their tea party. "About California, Bettina," he calls to her.

"What about it?"

"Is not time yet."

Mischa makes the mistake of leaving Bettina alone. At first it does not matter, she is exhausted from her biweekly therapy session and sits resting in the sun room of Brian Denlo, waiting for him. As her breathing grows calm, she becomes restless. She can't go upstairs and see Cathy as she generally does, Mischa told her when they came this morning that Cathy has been transferred to another hospital.

Thinking about it for the first time without distraction, Bettina is oddly uneasy. Cathy hadn't mentioned anything about it, the last time she was here. Why the sudden decision?

She'd like to think it was the first step back to the Avalon of Ara Sherwood's apartment up in the sky, but somehow the news is disturbing, as if Cathy is retreating into mist.

Bettina has never made the trip upstairs by herself, but she decides to go on up and see what she can find out from the other patients she knows on the floor. She has been memorizing numbers like lines of poetry, the poetry of freedom, and begins to go down the hall to the elevator, counting.

Eight . . . nine . . . that's right, here's the door to the library . . . *one . . . two . . .*

"Do you need a hand to get someplace, Bettina?" One of the nurses has spotted her, and called out to her.

"No, thanks. I'm managing."

She can do it. She can do almost anything she wants, if she tries, if she doesn't panic.

"How can you be so dumb? How can anybody be so dumb? Tell me you're kidding, Bettina. You really understand me, don't you, and you're kidding?"

"Damn you, Greg Weston, do you think I'd be letting you give me such a hard time if I understood?"

"*Cara* . . ."

"Pardon my French, Mom, but he makes me so mad. Come on, Greg, help me, will you?" and he said, as if he hadn't quite understood her, "Anybody can do this algebra. Anybody but an idiot."

The elevator doors close behind her and she stands leaning on the back wall as it climbs.

"Don't worry, *cara*. Girls don't have to be good in mathematics. I was simply dreadful. It doesn't matter. Nobody expects it of you. . . ."

And so she didn't do it. Brainwashed into being inferior. An unwitting conspiracy chiefly perpetuated by the victims, a gentle thoughtless demolishing conspiracy, as limiting as the skirts women made themselves wear. And now that all the math requirements for college are ended for Bettina, suddenly it is not difficult for her anymore, she can do any function she needs, she could have done it all along, it's the same brain, only she's no longer scared, no longer defeated. *Damn. Damn.*

The elevator stops at the third floor and she starts down the hall, tapping the side wall every once in a while with her rubber-tipped crutch foot to make sure she's going in a straight line.

... four ... five ... six ... seven ...

She is at the doorway to the room she used to share with Cathy. There doesn't seem to be anybody inside, the room exudes the peculiar echoing quality of emptiness. Bettina leans her hand on the door frame, inhaling the smell of the antiseptic that has cleaned away their germs. The small sounds of Cathy's rack, gone from the room, still haunt her head.

"Hey, Bettina! How are you doing? Long time no see."

It is Mr. Bellamy, eighty-three, with a broken hip. He has been walking the halls of Brian Denlo with a walker. He could go home if anybody wanted him.

"Hi, Mr. Bellamy. Are you okay? Good. Say, what can you tell me about Cathy?"

His answer is unexpected and shattering. He does not notice what he is doing to her as he talks on, glad for the importance the conversation gives him. He had talked to Cathy himself just the night before, nothing important, of course, just passing a few minutes before going to bed. They'd talked about the string beans they'd had at dinner, dreadful, the food has been getting worse since Bettina left.

Thinking it over afterwards, he realized Cathy had been kind of quiet, but nothing really noticeable. That's why it came as such a shock when he found out. The nurse found her in the morning, not a mark on her, nothing. It was just like she gave up breathing. Poor little thing. She was so pretty. But there probably were things there none of the rest of them ever understood. He never did like that fancy lady in the pant suits. . . .

The Studebaker heaves to a stop for a red light.

"Bettina? You are angry with me?"

"You're damned right, I'm angry with you."

"We think it best."

"Who's we? You and the godlike Dr. Greshak?"

"Is just to spare you pain."

They had thought she couldn't handle it. They are wrong. Her calmness is enormous, thuds without echoes. There's nothing inside her any more. Nothing.

She hears horns honking behind them. The light has changed and they should be moving on, but the Studebaker is old and tired and barely responds to Mischa's foot on the accelerator. The excitement behind them increases. Mischa responds angrily to the honking horns, to his own car. Bettina wishes she understood Russian.

The car heaves slightly, and then stalls. Mischa with effort gets the motor started again, but now the light has changed and they are stuck in the middle of the intersection, she can hear the cars trying to get around them as if they are a boulder in a stream. There is nothing to do but sit and laugh. And cry. . . .

He dries her face with a handkerchief. She realizes that he must finally have gotten the car out of the intersection, they are parked somewhere, and he is gently wiping her dry. He does not say anything. What could he say?

Cathy . . . Cathy . . . Cathy . . . Cathy Wallenstein. Twenty-one years old and dead. It is possible, after all, to will yourself dead. She feels enormously tired. She leans her head back on the seat of the car, aware of the ripped upholstery under the blanket Mischa has put over it.

He has started the motor again, and is

turning the car slowly back into the stream of traffic. "I'm sorry, Mischa."

"Is okay. I worry if you not feel bad for Cathy."

Who killed Cathy? Was she the one, deserting her? or was it the father, righteous, damning? or Ara Sherwood? or the screaming kids chanting "Cathy... Cathy..." or the fake golden crown, or the city that ate you up like it was starving....

They are all Caesar's assassins, each has struck a blow, only Bettina knows that hers was the fatal one, the blow of cowardice. She is overwhelmed with the most pervasive form of guilt, that of selfishness. She is her young mother who couldn't quite give her warm flesh to the cold dying man on the bed. She knows she took herself away from that room at Brian Denlo so that she would not have to cope with Cathy's problem, how much easier it had been to run away.

What good does it do to say that Cathy was going to die sooner or later, better sooner, she didn't have the strength for a long death. What a hypocrisy for the placation of the survivor!

"You okay, Bettina?"

"I'm alive, if that means anything. Cathy's dead, and I'm alive."

"Cathy dies long before you meet her. World

is full of people already dead."

"God, but you're Russian. . . ." She sighs and rolls down her window, hanging her hand down the outside of the Studebaker door. The wind shoves her fingers backwards, a delicate pushing sensation. She hears the yells of children at recess in a schoolyard. Life is going on. Life always goes on.

She sits with her head leaning against the old frame of the living room window, half-listening to the traffic passing outside, half-listening to Miss Moss reading from a privately published memoir her great-grandfather wrote about his experiences in the Civil War. Mischa has been in New York City all day straightening out his visa, and Miss Moss has most kindly offered to keep Bettina company.

Captain Orestes Moss has just ordered his 4th Pennsylvania Artillery down into the ravine where the stream runs through the heart of the Wilderness. It is springtime, early May, and there are pink gum trees in bloom, and wildroot, and violets.

Piero runs along the Arno at dawn in his blue sweatsuit with the symbol of Florence embroidered on his breast pocket, and lovely slender girls with long black hair down to their waists lean out of the windows of the ancient buildings to watch him pass, and does he now begin to turn to look back at them?

Corporal Warren Brubecker from Harrisburg is saying, "Sir, I think I smell smoke," and suddenly, the men are enveloped in flames, for the Wilderness is on fire.

There is a familiar sound intruding in the normal traffic pattern below, the noisy old Studebaker coming to the door of Miss Moss's house. Mischa is returning to her.

She will have to begin to think about Mischa one day soon Bettina will have to begin to think about Mischa.

Greg is leaving. Bettina is at the kitchen table, listening to him go. She had sensed his restlessness as they ate dinner together, and suggested that he take the night off. Oh God, he is running down the hall stairs as fast as he can go, escaping. She shoves aside the dishes and puts her sad head down on her arms on the table, sighing.

Now what? The clock is murmuring time *ick-a ick-a*. Greg has removed the plastic covering on the clock's face so that she can determine the position of the hands, but she doesn't have the energy or the spirit to go to the shelf and feel out the numbers.

She is extraordinarily tired. She cannot remember having done anything at all today, and yet she is completely exhausted. For an instant she considers crawling into bed, but forces herself away from that sweet thought, if she does that she will be slept out by the middle of the night and then there will be the rest of the night to spend without sleep, and that is worse. All time is not equal: insomnia time is infinitely longer than sunlit time.

Mischa is working the night shift, she won't see him tonight. What then for these hours that must be lived, TV without pictures? news and pop music radio? descent to Miss Moss's living room to sit in that deep and damp chair with cats climbing on her shoulders and that poor cracking voice telling another fairy-tale? But she must learn to be alone. Ultimately, the human soul goes to judgment alone.

There are always the dishes to be washed. Greg called to her as he left, telling her he would do them in the morning, but why? Salvation can walk in working shoes. Washing dishes is an act she has done for all of her life, she shouldn't have any trouble with it.

Greg comes home at midnight. She hears him moving in the kitchen, and then it seems to her that he stops at the door of her bedroom on his way to bed. She makes her breathing sound heavy and regular as sleep for as long as she thinks he's standing there. In no way is she ever going to let him know how many tears it took to wash clean a small invisible sinkful of dishes.

"What do you think of?" Mischa asks her.

She has been thinking of the sea. This is the kind of day when her mother would say suddenly, "Let's go swimming!" and off they would go, she and her mother and Greg, to Island Beach State Park, crowded, noisy, littered, but affordable, and beautifully edged by the sea.

"Okay, we go to the sea today."

"Oh, no, Mischa. Not today."

"And why not today?"

There are a hundred reasons why not. It is early in the year, and the seashore will be cold. It is quite a long distance to drive from here. They have other things they should be doing.

"Bettina, you cannot keep from other people for rest of your life. We go to the sea today. I go now to the deli and buy us some food, and then we go to the sea."

* * *

They sat under their umbrella, slowly unpacking lunch. Around them everyone was laughing and yelling and running as always, and the sea roared in to the shore with sunlight trapped yellow in the peaks of its waves, calling them, *Come on, come on, it's good today*

but their father was dead, was dead, they felt no warmth, they heard noise without joy, somewhat resentful that their mother had brought them here to this cheerful place when they should be mourning

and she was setting out enormous quantities of food, more food than they could have eaten if they had been twenty roaring athletes instead of one brittly brave woman and her two disconsolate children. Bettina held the plate her mother gave her, receiving spoonfuls of potato salad, and boiled eggs, and corn chips, and the olives had bobbled on the plate as in a macabre dance.

* * *

"Sù, sù," their mother said. "Your father would want us to go on," and so Bettina had put the food in her mouth and swallowed it and afterwards vomited it all back up, trying not to make a lot of noise and attract the attention of the other bathers sitting nearby. Her mother had not said anything, but had quietly buried the vomit in the sand.

Suddenly Bettina is smelling the sea, salt and fish and weed, and it seems to her she hears the wail of gulls through the open window of Mischa's rumbling car. They must be passing through the little summer towns of row on row of flimsy and drab identical cottages, the main streets lined with quick-food joints, pinball emporiums, package stores, souvenir shops. Everything would still be at rest now before the summer influx, nothing refurbished yet for the summer trade, tawdry, chipped at by the winter wind, unbelievably unrelievedly ugly, she knows them all without seeing them.

Mischa parks the car in the main lot of the park and helps her out. "Grab my shirt," he tells her, as he loads his arms with the things they have brought with them. She lets him lead her across the parking lot, poling along with her crutch slightly behind him so they can look like the usual clinging sweethearts, casual glances will not identify her necessity. They turn the corner of the refreshment stand with its smell of hotdogs and the murmur of people and suddenly she is tasting sea wind.

Her father was carrying her on his shoulders across the sand into the ocean, her strong young father, not yet ill, and she was shrieking in phony terror, clutching his straight brown hair with both hands, her knees strangling him. He was laughing and she was completely in love with him as he walked her into the splashing sea, she would have let him take her off the end of the earth.

Her hair has been growing, and the fragile scarred area at the back of her head is covered with longer hair from the top of her scalp, held down with bobby pins. She touches her face quickly, but has no idea whatsoever if she looks passable. "Are people staring at me?" she whispers to Mischa. "Are they looking?"

"Sure, they're looking. You're one

pretty girl."

"I can imagine."

The foot of her crutch digs into the sand, and her cast is dragging. In spite of her most concentrated effort, she quickly finds herself lagging behind Mischa, pulling his shirt away from his body, finally letting go of him and stopping.

"We rest for a minute," he says, and she stands there panting with her effort, sweated, desperately wanting to cry at her incredible weakness, remembering how she used to be able to run for a whole day on this beach without feeling anything like this order of exhaustion.

The brisk sea wind chills her as she rests, and she can hear the familiar voices of children in wide concentric circles about her. Slowly it seems to her that immediately around her there is silence, people must be staring at her, she feels a flight of hostile arrows coming at her from all directions.

"Oh, Mischa," she whispers desperately. "Please, let's go back. . . ."

"Come on," he tells her. "Come on," and she has to push on across the sand after him. She is angry with him, but vulnerable and without choice, she cannot go anywhere without him, she must obey him, totally his victim.

Her breath is choking her, she is tired beyond imagining from the effort of pulling her enormously heavy leg across the sand, she is crying. God, but she hates him! He's always pushing her a little beyond what she wants to do, beyond dignity, beyond exhaustion. All through the months of her therapy at Brian Denlo, he has hounded her with his, "Come on, come on, just a little more, you can do it. . . ." and she'd scream at him, "You can say that because it isn't you having to do it, God, I wish it was you. . . ." and he'd answer her calmly, "Enough talk. Come on, come on. . . ."

and so she follows him across the sand, thinking how much she wants to bite and scratch him, hit him with a club with a nail in it, no human being should so force another, she should be able to choose the speed of her own recovery, if she was old enough to drive a car, old enough to get herself into this predicament in the first place, dammit, she should be free. . . .

She trips over something, her own leg, probably, and sits down heavily, panting, not caring if people are staring at her, not caring about anything. "I'm not moving one goddamned inch," she tells him.

She hears him go away. When he returns, he

has found a good place for them, and set down their beach supplies. He gives her the crutch to hold and then lifts her in his arms, staggering with the weight. She has a moment of glee that he is suffering, *Let him find out what it feels like, after what he made me do* . . . but almost immediately, hearing the sound of his breath gasping audibly in his chest, she is ashamed of herself. All of this, all of it, he's doing for her, this gentle stranger.

"Sorry to be such a bitch," she tells him, and puts her head against his. His hair is wet with sweat.

Finally the two of them tumble down together onto the blanket he has spread on the sand. They lie quietly on their stomachs for a long time, his arm around her shoulders. It is very peaceful; they are far beyond the crowds, the human voices are lonely echoes borne on the wind. The wind carries the tiny grains of sand up over the edge of the blanket in a fine coating that spreads like film over them, she hears the individual grains tumbling and running, they make an unbelievably clear sound.

It comes to her that she has never listened like this before. She has not known the wind, the hundred winds, she has lived with wind for all of her life and never listened to it.

Mischa sits up. "I think maybe I swim, okay?" he asks her.

"Take a few strokes for me. . . ."

She lies very still after he is gone, with her good arm over her eyes, listening to incredible sounds, the heavy wash of the incoming waves, of course, but also the small afterfoam snapping its bubbles, the quick nervous run of the screeching pipers pursuing the waves, the panting of a crab under the sand as it peeks up its little hole at the sun, the sinewy bending of tough sea grass, her own heartbeat thudding evenly like an unending drip of mineraled water from an underground stalactite reaching down to its other-self stalagmite.

The unbearable itching of her leg intrudes on her small sensory experiences, and she sits up, impatiently feeling around for something to thrust down into her cast. Mischa has straightened out a coat hanger for this purpose, but it is at Greg's apartment. Dr. Greshak has promised her that in two weeks the cast will be off; two weeks is too long.

She finds a plastic fork in the hamper and thrusts it down into her cast, as far as she can reach. This is a strange need, on the edge of hysteria, she wants to tear the skin, needing the relief of suffering, itch is a special kind of pain like desire, like sex, like phobia and finally, hurting, she lies down again, a small trickle of blood inside her cast, she has tortured herself into relief, welcoming the discomfort, anything is better than that hellish itch.

"Okay, Bettina?" Mischa is asking her.

He is back, standing just beyond the edge of the blanket, she can hear the drip of water from his jeans hitting the sand.

"How was it?"

"Good. Cold, but good."

"The water is warmer in the Pacific, you know."

He hesitates. "Is okay," he says finally. "Russian is not afraid of a little cold."

She reaches up to him and he comes to her, embracing her, his body cool and wet from the sea. She puts her forehead against his, whispering, "Oh, Mischa. Did I make you up because I needed you so badly?"

and he repeats, "Did I make you up, Bettina, because I needed you. . . ."

Mischa comes up the stairs with a letter just arrived from Italy. She takes it to put it as usual with the others in the drawer, still unopened, but then she hesitates.

"Mischa, do you think maybe . . ."

"Yes? What do you ask me, Bettina?"

She fingers the letter, tempted, afraid. Perhaps she could have him look at this one, just this one, not reading it to her, not telling her everything it says, just finding out whether this is the letter that will tell her, tactfully, politely, that there is somebody else now in Piero's life, *dear Bettina, I am sorry but* . . .

It has been such a long time, time enough for seasons to change, time enough for her hair to grow again, time enough for even the deepest of emotions to diminish for lack of sustenance. Is love after all inert like stone, or is it living like a plant that must be carefully nurtured or die? What does she have the right to expect of it? And truly, what is love? We scatter the word in all directions, *I love your dress, I love lobster (steak) (chocolate pudding)*, and, for God so loved the world that He sent His only begotten son . . .

Piero said, in the long ago, "Love is whatever is needed." But that was an abstract, spoken with their lips inches apart and waiting. What was it that she and Piero shared, a trivial love based on youth and sexual attraction, and summertime in a beautiful land? Agony has drawn a heavy black line between her and the child that handsome boy fell in love with. Would he still love her if he knew her now, and would she love him?

Reason tells her this, but she will not let herself think it yet, for Piero has always been the hidden reward she promises herself if she is a good girl and does all of her unspeakable exercises, he is the cap at the top of the pole, the ride in Apollo's chariot after poling the Styx, and she has to have that lure to continue through the hell

and so she slams the drawer shut upon his letter, crying out to Mischa, "Never mind! Never mind...."

She comes awake screaming. Whatever dream she was pursuing is gone. All that exists in the whole world for her now, this instant, is the wild knot of pain in her leg. It is so intense that she is immediately soaked in sweat.

At once she stifles the sound of her pain, not wanting to waken Greg. Poor Greg, no need for him to witness this. Again.

She desperately wants to rub the knotted muscles, to undo the tight bundle, but knows from experience that makes it worse. All she can do is hold her breath and pray, *Dear God please dear God please* she must be getting ten years off from purgatory for each of these episodes ... *Oh God, fifteen....*

Slowly, slowly, the agony subsides, the memory so extreme that she still gasps from it after the actuality lessens. Finally, it is over. She lies very still, not daring to move, feeling echoes of pain in her muscles, fatigue, acute awareness, but the spasm is over.

It is the very heart of the night. There isn't a sound anywhere except the clock she has carried to her room, not traffic, not voices, not even the usual faraway dog. Everything, everyone, is asleep. She reaches for the faceless clock, and fingers out the time: 2:15. Half a night used up and no sleep left in her to bring her safely to morning.

Sighing, she gets up and, gingerly using the healing leg, hobbles out to the kitchen in an uneven motion that concentrates on her good leg. She fills a glass with water, not thirsty, but making herself take a sip to justify being there, and then carries the glass back toward her room, pausing at the door to Greg's bedroom, listening to his heavy breathing.

"Greg..."

He continues to breathe steadily, unhearing. What, after all, can he do for her? They have already had their conversation about the meaning of pain.

* * *

"You're being simplistic, Bettina. Medieval. This pain isn't you paying the price for having the cast off. You don't have to buy that, it's just something that has logically happened because enough time has passed. The reason you're having the pain is because your muscles are knotting, they've been inactive for all this time, and now you're moving them again. Period."

The religion they grew up with was like the kid who never told a lie because he didn't know it was possible to tell anything but the truth. When he realized that he could get away with lying and not be found out, most of the time, then truth became something else for him. They are adults now, and they must consider the possibility that whatever God is, He doesn't give a damn about them. She of all people should be able to think that.

"You talk a good fight about being

free of your upbringing, Bettina, of not conforming, but honestly, are you really thinking, or are you just perpetuating?"

"I believe what's right for me," she said, but she couldn't continue the argument, she didn't have her hands on God, either. God peek-a-booed with her constantly, He disappeared into perfect hiding places while she counted up to her one hundred

and she had no idea of what He wanted of her, or if He did want her or even if He was at all. Perhaps she had been patterned, as Greg thought, in childhood, to see God where He is not and even if He is not

but at least she is still wondering.

She knows she has lost Greg, he is now as remote as royalty. As children, they had the loyalty of loneliness, the conspiracy of poverty. It did not matter what tragedy occurred, he was available. Now he is an adult. Their blood ties cannot be obliterated, but the friendship is gone. Or maybe, in all honesty, it never was, it just looked as if it existed because it was convenient that it should.

The first flush of Greg's worry over her has passed and now there is a strained patience in his relationship with her, she is the somewhat backward child who has gotten herself into serious trouble and has ended up being singularly tiring. He knows his obligations but they have lasted too long, he is aware of what they have done to the quality of his life.

Because they are now strangers, she goes back to her bed with her unwanted glass of water without calling him again.

She sits in a chair under the trees in the spring out-of-doors listening to Mischa's power mower somewhere in the distance as he cuts the grass on the estate where he now lives. He told her he grew tired of the bed behind the dark curtain in the hospital basement, and that is why he has made a deal with a wealthy family named O'Rourke now away in Hawaii to take care of the grounds of their estate in exchange for use of a small gatehouse left over from more

European days. She suspects he has done it so that he will have this kind of a place to bring her.

It is very peaceful here, far from the city air that comes through the open window of Miss Moss's cat-haunted house. The scent of the cut grass stabs the heart with its familiarity, of nighttime walks in bare feet in the moonlight, of Greg behind their recalcitrant mower cutting lawns for the neighbors and hating it but needing the money, of being sick and having her father wave to her every time he pushed the power mower past her window....

She is supposed to be working on her Braille. Mischa has told her harshly, is she perhaps able to make permanent blindness any less of a possibility by refusing to acknowledge it? At least, if she has capability in the Braille, the darkness will not be so black, she will not be so afraid of it. In a high place in her brain, in the province of the intellect, cold and rarified as the space between the stars, she knows he is right, and so she has been trying, but the flesh hurts and the blood is warm and the shadows and sunlight she knows with her skin are making her retreat into a lethargy of semi-memory, semi-dream.

Slowly, she becomes aware of the tears cutting her cheeks. Was it then a sad dream?

She does not even remember what she was thinking; everything lately seems unbearably sad, she is always on the way to tears.

Mischa calls to her, "Come, pretty lady, I take you away with me on my white horse." He has been watching her and has come back to rescue her from her own dragons. She feels him caress her short hair before he picks her up and puts her on his knees on the seat of the mower.

"Oh, Mischa, you're so good to me," she whispers. She puts her arms around his neck and kisses his cheek through his short beard, wanting him to forget California, she is terrified that he will remember California, and so she tells him, teasing him timidly, "You know, I think I'm half in love with you."

He shifts the gears of the mower, saying, "Oh? Which half?" and carries her on his roaring iron stallion across the spring lawn through the bee-humming afternoon.

She has no idea what time it is, but it is late. There are almost no cars left on the streets, everyone is neatly clothed in special garb for sleeping and filed into a comfortable box for the night. She should be there, too; she did in fact undress and put on her night clothing and climb into her bed, but that was a long time ago, long before the hours and hours of listening to the clock *ick-a*ing, of waiting for the sound of Greg's car to park at the curb downstairs, long before her panic.

Greg doesn't always come home at night anymore. She knows he's having an affair with somebody. They never quite talk about it, but there's something about the way he sounds, as if he's always smiling in his belly. Maybe if she weren't at the apartment, the girl would be spending the night with Greg here above Miss Moss's uncomprehending head. But little sister is living here now, and so Greg goes elsewhere.

He has not called tonight to let her know he will not be home. Usually he does, although there have been a few times when she has waked up in the morning, aware that she is still alone in the apartment, that the whole night has passed and he is not home yet. She does not worry about him in the daytime, knowing that if he were in trouble, someone else would find him out there and take care of him. But in the darkness, she's the only one in the whole world who knows that he has not come in yet, she's the one who should be telling somebody that he might have crashed into a pole somewhere on an uninhabited stretch of road, he might be dying for want of her sending help.

And so, as the hours of waiting pass, she has

come down the stairs from the apartment, step by step. She sits in her nightgown on one step, head against the wall, restless after a time and having to descend another step, and another, until she has reached the landing with the front door beyond.

Everything is still in the house. Miss Moss lies unmoving like a skeleton in her virginal bed and her animals stalk her rooms so soundlessly that only God knows that they are moving, a strange small army of bodies leaping in and out through the open window.

Bettina opens the front door and goes out onto the porch, guiding herself with her hands along the right-hand railing, sitting down finally on weathered boards so old and shrivelled she can feel the separations between them in her skin through her nightgown as she seats herself leaning against the balustrade, her knees under her chin, her feet holding down the hem of her gown.

It is warm outside, a fat summer night. The air is lissome, caressing, and carries on it the sound of insects, a hundred thousand million insects each making an infinitesimal sound, the combined accumulation rising like a shriek. She rests her head on her knees, thinking, *they don't care that I'm here. Nobody cares.*

A car is coming. She hears the beginning of

its sound somewhere off to the right, turning from the major highway onto this street. Her heart begins to race with listening. Will the car turn again at any one of the half-dozen small roads lined with houses before it reaches here, does it belong somewhere else, or is Greg finally coming home, safe? *Please, please, come this way....* She hears the increasing sound of the car coming, it makes it past the temptation of the other roads, it comes and comes, she can almost allow herself to feel relief

but then it flashes on past Miss Moss's house and goes down the street and off into black space and finally she doesn't even hear it any more.

Almost immediately there's another car coming from the other direction and she can hope again, but that car also comes and goes and the night is still again except for the scream of the insects. Then there are no more cars for a very long time.

How alone she is. It seems to her that she is in a subterranean Venetian prison, waiting for the tide to come in on her and drown her, and she sits unmoving, she does not try to stand up and buy herself a few minutes of life, she sits unmoving there behind the slats of Miss Moss's porch railing and waits for death to begin....

She must have drowsed. She wakes slowly

with the soreness in her bones of having stayed too long in an uncomfortable position. What woke her? She listens to the night. It sounds different, now, it breathes, the insects are very still, she is hearing the movement of waking birds

and Mischa is coming.

In the silent predawn, all traffic is absent except the rattling distant panting of the yellow Studebaker, she hears it coming, and that is what wakened her, she was waiting for it, she willed it to come to her with her under-soul and when it obeys she wakens from the blank sleep with which she was protecting herself.

She hears the car stop in front of the house, she hears the driver's door slam and there are footsteps on the cement walk. Almost without volition, she stands up and waits. She hears his steps stop; he must have spotted her.

"Where do you get such ugly nightgown?" he asks her.

"It was a gift," she answers, her voice breaking, and runs to him, stumbling in that stupid nightgown, gathering tiny splinters in her feet, running to his voice, knowing that he will catch her before she runs off the steps, before she reaches danger, before she is lost, he will take care of her.

She clutches him with all her strength,

crying desperately, the tears of worthlessness. He holds her, murmuring. She doesn't distinguish the words, or even the language. It doesn't matter. Somebody is holding her. Somebody from the world beyond her black little shell knows about her.

"Greg is still out?" he asks her finally.

"Mischa, is it Hoss?"

He doesn't say anything. Oh God, Hoss. *They don't even like each other*. But they are male and female, and for as long as that is sufficient, Greg will leave. She thinks she is angry with them for so carelessly allowing her to suffer, but that isn't her emotion: Now that she isn't alone any more, now that there is no more chance for guilt, what she feels is a continuation of disillusionment: *Oh Greg, oh Hoss, at least if it had meant something. . . .*

"How come you're here, Mischa?" she asks him.

He had seen her light still on at midnight when he drove home from work. It bothered him. He'd gone to bed but couldn't sleep, wondering. Finally, he'd come. He says it all casually, as if it is unimportant, but she knows that this house is not on his route home, he must pass this way to check on her. She sighs and leans her head on his shoulder. "You don't have to keep worrying about me," she says.

"I've got to learn to manage on my own."

"Is not issue. Look, Bettina, I am thinking. I want you to come to live with me at my cottage. Now. Without going back into house. I come later, and get your things."

She is not sure what he is saying to her. "Don't tell me you're propositioning me," she whispers.

"What does that mean, propositioning?"

"Oh, God." It's almost funny. A language difficulty in such a situation. "It means . . . are you asking . . . that we become lovers. . . ."

And he answers her, "Ah. Yes. I am asking that we become lovers."

The birds are coming alive around her. She can hear them flutter and respond to one another up in the trees, the rooftops, the sky, she is surrounded by birds. She is so alive that she can feel the tiny hairs on her arms stirring in the rising morning breeze. She feels the warmth of Mischa's body, not quite touching. She thinks to hear his heartbeat.

For the first time, she is aroused by him. For hundreds and thousands of times he has moved and carried her and had his arms around her and she has not responded to his body, they have been two ballet dancers locked in intimate balance without sex, and now, now, not touching, she is enflamed by him. And yet, this had to be, the different magnetic poles have been coming closer and closer, they have reached the critical point of attraction, the halves come together.

She knows she should be afraid, and she should be remembering, but she lets herself go down the rabbithole. She holds on to him, to his familiar bones, and he is kissing her, for the first time since Piero a man has her lips, and she is reacting to him.

"But I'm so ugly," she whispers, needing his denial. "I can't take kindness, it would kill me."

He kisses her more passionately, crying out, "You are beautiful, you are daylight . . . people turn when I walk with you, they turn to look at you . . . I love you so much I cannot stay away. . . ." and his voice cracks, he almost cannot speak, he pauses, gulping air between phrases. He gives her beauty, he gives her value, he gives her himself, and she is no longer afraid.

There is an uncertain rattling of the lock of the front door, the silent gallop of ghosts pass them as Miss Moss opens the door and her animals escape her. "Oh, is it you, my dears?" she murmurs sleepily. "I heard someone out here and thought it was company."

She does not appreciate the incongruity of

the moment. She stands in the doorway in her ancient nightclothes looking unwonderingly at Bettina in her nightgown being kissed by Mischa, and expects company that never comes to arrive at five in the morning.

"Miss Moss, I take Bettina home with me," says Mischa, picking Bettina up in his arms. She feels him trembling. Somehow, that excites her, it is an unconscious movement, completely sincere, he is truly aroused by her.

"That's nice, my dears," says Miss Moss's squeaky voice. "Just don't forget to put out all the lights."

They don't want to go back into the apartment. There is a wildness to them, an impatience to get away. "Greg will pay the bill," says Mischa.

That tickles Bettina. Greg will pay the bill. God, but he owes. And then she doesn't think about Greg anymore. Mischa takes her down the stairs, he takes her away. Because she is beautiful, she curls herself around him. Because she is beautiful, she goes away with him.

She comes awake, sweating; for an instant, unthinking, it seems to her she is still the child who was afraid of falling asleep. Memory increases her terror; she is indeed Bettina, but grown up and blind.

"Mischa..."

"Ummmmm?"

"Hold me."

More asleep than awake, he cradles her in his arms, he rests his chin on her head and drowses off to sleep again. She listens to his even heartbeat; their skin together engenders a sweat that feels cold as he relaxes and separates from her. At once she leans against him again, needing the contact.

She can hear a mouse running in the wall of the gatehouse kitchen, a fieldmouse, probably, that has wandered in during the cold of winter, and, having tasted the sweet temptations of man's food, is willing to risk annihilation for them, she envisions the country mouse and the city mouse, dressed in Dickensian clothes, in a children's book of fables. . . .

She is safe in Mischa's arms, but beyond him is this unfamiliar room, a room of strangers. She listens to its sighing ghosts, to its restless unborn, the room is filled with movement, busy spirits that do not threaten because she is not alone

and Mischa breathes, with small pauses between each inhalation, frightening instants when she is terrified that he has died, and has escaped her

she creeps closer to him, feeling the emanation of warmth and of life from his young body, she is photosensitive and he is the sun. . . .

All day long the rain comes down, summer rain smelling of distant cement sidewalks and black dirt made wet, and she remembers the extraordinary brilliance of green leaves and grass in the sunlight after a heavy rain.

It has been a good day. First they went to the A&P for some groceries, and she held on to the shopping cart as Mischa pushed it. A child running past said, "Hi!" to her and never noticed anything.

Then Bettina cooked a dinner, a real dinner, not the usual cold cuts from the deli that are their way of life, but roast chicken with rosemary and instant mashed potatoes and a salad, accompanied by quite a lot of white wine.

Now the day is ending and the rain still falls. They have been sitting together in a lumpy old chair Mischa bought for this tiny living room for a dollar from Good Will Industries, an enormous monster hidden by a stretched hand-knit afghan (seventy-five cents). Because it is now cool with evening and the accumulation of a long day of dampness, they have the afghan pulled around them to keep them warm while he tells her folk tales about the Baba Yaga, the Russian witch who lives in a dreadful cottage surrounded by stakes on top of which are human skulls with glowing eyes

and pretty peasant girls must outwit her to get their loves

and always do

and the rain falls steadily on the roof and they are safe and warm wrapped in leaves in a tiny walnut shell floating on a river.

"Tell me another," she says, as he ends his last story. "Please, Mischa, tell me another," and he pauses, thinking, and then starts again.

He tells her the tale of a poor woodchopper's son who falls in love with a beautiful princess who is being held, sleeping, under a wicked spell, by the Baba Yaga. He follows his love through all kinds of dreadful places, suffering the most anguishing experiences, to an enormous white bone tower standing in the middle of a barren plain.

The boy does not know how to get inside the tower, but because he shares his last crust of bread with a starving bird, he is given three magic stones on which to wish. "Be careful what you ask for, my brother," the bird tells the woodchopper's son sadly, but the boy doesn't stop to listen to what the bird is trying to tell him, he hides two of the stones in his pocket and throws the other over his shoulder as he has been instructed, and wishes, "That I may get into the tower."

He uses the second stone to wish for protection from the Baba Yaga once he is inside the tower; the third he saves to use to rescue the sleeping princess, whom he knows lies at the top of the tower.

The boy works for the Baba Yaga for months and months, washing the dreadful floors covered with vomit and blood and filth, and sometimes it is almost too much for him, he wants to lie down and die. He is so tired, and everything around him is so incredibly ugly, it is as if he has opened a door on hell.

"Oh, Mischa," murmurs Bettina unhappily, knowing what he is telling her, but he goes on as if he hasn't heard her, talking about how when the woodchopper's son is most discouraged, he makes himself remember the beautiful princess, and goes on.

One night he tricks the Baba Yaga into drinking too much vodka by telling her he can drink more than she can. When it is his turn he pours the vodka into the sack of a goat's belly he has hidden under his jacket, until finally she falls down as one dead under the table. Then he races up the stairs to the tower, with the dreadful hordes of the Baba Yaga following him like a nightmare. He reaches the sleeping princess, and with the last bit of energy left in his body, throws the third white stone over his shoulder, whispering weakly, "That the princess and I may be safely away from this place."

At once they are in a sunlit field near his father's hut in the forest, he and the princess are safe. The boy is overjoyed, thinking he has gotten his heart's desire, but as the days pass, he comes to understand the sadness of his brother bird: no matter how much he loves the princess, he does not know how to make her wake up for him. She continues to sleep, dreaming of a rich prince in fine garments she had known before the spell was cast on her.

"Oh, Mischa. That's not true."

"Is not?"

"No. I love you. I love you." She embraces him in guilty anguish, ashamed that she has caused him pain, clutching him the more because she does not know for sure that what she says is true.

She is sitting on the grass. She can feel the dampness of earth, and smells ancient leaves and flowers. With great concentration, she is tipping and tailing string beans for dinner.

Never has she been so aware of the slightly furry texture of the beans, through her fingers she seems to have put the slender rods under a very strong lens so that she peers close-up at the skins.

The cleaned beans drop into the colander, each one making a different sound according to where it falls; she listens and listens with constant surprise, all these little experiences have always existed only she did not know them, she ran past masterpieces in too great a hurry, a mad rush to . . . what?

Oh God, if she can ever see again, she will never miss another twilight with pinks seeping up mauves and finally purples from the darkening earth, space chromatography, she will never miss another rainstorm, another midnight, surely she will never sleep again.

Something seems to be happening to her: it is as if she has crashed through a barrier into a new level of existence, she is seeing, as in, "I see," says the blind man . . . *I see . . . says the blind man. . . .*

She feels an incredible lightness, a loss of reality, of weight. Surely, in an instant she will rise into the air and float away and be lost among the stars, the infinite violet stars. *Maybe I'm being born, born at last.*

Mischa is weeding within reach of her hand.

Every once in a while she touches him, following him as he shifts along the flowerbed. She puts out her hand again, knowing he is there, but needing the reassurance of flesh on flesh. Immediately he responds to her, caressing her hair quickly with the back of his hand so as not to touch her with his dirty palm.

Mischa Mischa Mischa

She seizes him, clutching his bare body under his unbuttoned shirt with both arms, she presses her cheek upon his beating heart, pursuing him, *Mischa,* to where he is hidden within that strong young body

for he is what is happening to her

and she wants to tell him what she feels, she wants to say it for him, God knows he deserves it, but there are still echoes in her soul

and so finally she says, "You're putting on weight, do you know that? You're not so damned skinny any more, my cooking must agree with you."

He takes her to a fine restaurant for dinner. She does not want to go, to risk public embarrassment when it is so easy to stay home, but he drags her, in spite of herself, toward normalcy.

The dinner goes well. There is an excitement, a joy, to being in a crowd, that she had forgotten. The steady level of sound of people talking and laughing around them is like an unnoticed baritone sax making a background to the melody, the moment is quicker because of it.

Every once in a while he touches her lightly, her hand, her cheek, her hair, in an almost unconscious caress as he talks to her

waking birds, lethargy, contentment, a hollow of warmth in the covers as she lay half asleep, smiling because he was tracing her forehead, her nose, her lips with his fingertips, and it tickled

she sops up his love like broth in bread, like rain on sunfried earth

and it comes to her how much she is at peace, here, now, with him. It is a life that can go on forever. She can have his children, other blind women have raised children. For the first time in an eternity of darkness, it seems to her that she has a future.

And then she notices something, she notices his silence. It is like a warning bell tolling danger, and she responds to it, that distant clapping of despair. *Oh, God, Mischa, don't say the next thing. Leave it here, right where we are now, this beautiful place where we are dwelling, you and I....*

But through the laughter of strangers she hears him say, "I spoke to Dr. Greshak yesterday...." and it is time, time for the surgery Dr. Greshak has promised her, the surgery of trial, with two possibilities. The rough old man has asked Mischa, *Is she ready for defeat?* and Mischa must have answered, *She can live with it,* but she is trembling, for she is afraid, afraid, and suddenly she knows that she's not afraid of darkness, but of light.

She sits on the wide stone sill of the bay window of the living room, clutching her knees. She is washed in sunlight; surely, finally, her bones are warm.

It must be twilight now in Florence. Cars run on the pink Boulevard Lungarno. The air-conditioned buses are dragging in tired tourists from San Gimignano, from Pisa, from Siena, and Piero carries a cup of *espresso* out onto the balcony of the Ferrari apartment to watch the sculls passing below on the Arno.

She sees his face undiminished. Perhaps it is

because there is the possibility that she will see again. A part of herself that she has denied, submerged, suppressed, breaks loose, and it is as if nothing at all has happened in the interim, they two are still waiting for each other. . . .

"You think of him."

She did not know he was watching her and is immediately overcome with guilt. "No, Mischa, I'm not. . . ."

"Don't worry. Is to be expected."

"Is dumb, that's what it is. I'd only be hurting you. Piero's undoubtedly had three girlfriends by now, you know these Latin lovers."

It sounds forced, even to her, and doesn't evoke the hoped-for response from Mischa. There is a silence, and when he speaks again, his voice is odd and tight. "Bettina, there is something I must tell you."

"About what?"

"About Piero."

"Will you please stop being so damned noble about him? What is it, don't you want me any more?"

"Bettina! Is just that you should know, you will find out. . . ."

"What?"

"Piero comes to hospital, to St. Mary's. Greg calls him when you are hurt and he comes, across the ocean. He doesn't let you know he is here, you do not want him, but he comes, and he watches, he waits."

Her emotions are fragmenting in every direction. Piero had come. The man crying beside her when she was in Intensive Care was Piero, and when she was in the room with Mrs. Callaghan she had indeed smelled his aftershave lotion, she felt his kiss.

"How long was he . . ."

"Until you recover from kidney repair."

She had heard him calling her. He hung on to her. Was he the reason she came back? Or was Mischa?

There is a strange emotion in her soul, a sudden unexpected relief. The unrecognized sense of betrayal, that he had not cared enough to disregard her desperate protestations, is gone. He did come, he came and stayed with her, silently, until she was out of danger.

"Why didn't anybody tell me?"

"At first they are afraid, you get excited, you hurt yourself. Later on, no one tells . . ."

No one told because of him. "Well, it doesn't really matter," she says. "It doesn't change anything."

"You are sure of that? In your heart, you are sure?"

She takes his hand in both of hers, kissing it

quickly. "Yes, Mischa. Yes!"

"Then you are no longer afraid of his letters."

"Why should I be?"

"So, now is time to read them."

"Mischa . . ."

"Yes?"

"Nothing."

She hears him go to the drawer, open it, get out the letters. Slowly, slowly, she slides down to the floor, sitting cross-legged, with her palms upwards in the position of meditation, in the position of prayer. What is there to pray for? After what she and Mischa have been through together, the letters from Piero can hurt, but they cannot make a difference.

The letters are undiminishedly passionate. How much of the emotion in the later ones is Italian literary expression? She is immediately ashamed for thinking that about Piero, but there is no way she can know solid truth, and that hurts.

"He wants you, Bettina. Blind or with sight, he wants you."

There is a pain in her chest as if a subterranean rock has cracked deep within her, and an enormous unseen river is flowing through, a river of tears that escapes sadly from her blank eyes and falls onto her lap, she can feel the wet spots in her jeans.

She is haunted with the vision of herself walking into that exquisite white Ferrari apartment, blind Bettina knocking down unseen plants, banging into people, apologizing and apologizing ... Piero would tell her again and again that it does not matter, Ina Ferrari and Stefano in his sexy pants would tell her it does not matter, but she would not see, she would never see Piero's gray eyes, and because she wouldn't, she would never know for sure whether he was lying.

"If you can see, what then, Bettina?"

She jumps up quickly, tottering from the suddenness of it: because she cannot orient herself by sight, it takes her longer to gain her balance. She catches hold of his shoulder, saying, "It won't make a lot of difference, and you know it, you black Russian, you. Come on, let's see if we can put together some sort of a dinner. Did we remember to take chopped meat out of the freezer?"

"No." And then he says, his voice wavering slightly, "I think maybe tonight we eat caviar. And drink champagne."

"But I don't like caviar."

He laughs then and grabs her up in his arms, laughing and yelling, "Tonight I eat caviar! Tonight you drink champagne!" and she holds on to him, pierced by his delight, she buries her face in his shoulder, not breathing.

There is a strange sensation in her head, her faraway head. *Damn you, Dr. Greshak, I want to be . . . Bettina. . . .*
Her head swings and swings and she feels a growing nausea

Greg held her hands and swung her around and around. "Don't let go!" she was screaming. "Don't let go!" She stared at his belt buckle, feeling sick to her stomach, feeling her feet flying through the air, in a moment she would hit a tree with her feet, hit a passing stranger, her brother would surely let go of her hands and she would leave the spinning earth and fall into the sun

too many times
around and around and around, she feels the violent sickness of her stomach, she wants to cry out, *Please, Greg, no more. . . .*

* * *

Her eyes were closed and she was leaning her forehead against Piero's throat, letting him take her where he would. *Take me to hell if you want: as long as you are with me, I'll go* . . . and in the apartment behind them the foolish voice on the record was singing, *amami . . . amami. . . .*

She retches and swallows instinctively. God. She shouldn't have eaten that last bite of Mischa's apple. Someone puts the familiar metal dish under her chin, a woman smelling of nylon and softener. Bettina retches, but nothing comes up.

Two glasses of water
hole as big as Grand Central Station
oh God, oh God.

There's a pain in her head as if someone is trying to yank the two halves apart with his hands
and succeeding
a truck is driving through her head.

"Bettina!" Dr. Greshak is saying. It seems to her that he's tapping her cheek, insistently. "Bettina!"

"Wha . . ."

"Ah, good. She's coming around. The

operation is over, Bettina. The operation is over."

She swallows. The operation is over.

The pain is tremendous, it is the only reality. "It hurts," she whispers desperately. "You can't believe how much it hurts," and she is begging.

"We'll give you something in a minute," says Dr. Greshak. "First, let's see how it goes."

How what goes? She tries to remember, but the pain is too intense, she is falling through pain as thick as mud.

"Dr. Adams is with me, Bettina. He's the man who operated on you. Bettina? Do you hear me?"

She hears him. *Dr. Adams, the man who...* Sweat starts up under her eyes with remembrance. The operation is over. The operation... "Mischa?" she whispers in panic, reaching out her hand, hitting someone who retreats.

"I am here, Bettina. I am here."

Mischa's hands grip both of hers, his strong familiar hands. She hasn't the strength to hold on to him. "Don't let go," she whispers. "Please, don't let go...."

they are running her to the operating room because her kidney has ruptured. *Please, don't let go....*

"Bettina, I'm Dr. Adams. I'm going to take the pads off your eyes now, and you tell us what you see. All right?"

The beginning of the rest of her life. Her heartbeat is so rapid it suffocates.

"Bettina?"

"Yes. I understand. Go ahead."

"Now, I have to tell you before we begin, we don't have much hope for the right eye. You mustn't panic if nothing's changed."

"But the left eye looks good, baby," says Dr. Greshak. "And one out of two isn't bad, is it?" He's gasping slightly.

"We'll start with the right eye," says Dr. Adams. "Okay, I'm taking off the pad. Tell me. Do you see any improvement, any at all?"

Slowly, she opens the eye he's uncovered. She feels the sudden stir on her exposed wet eyeball. Her eye is open.

"Anything?"

She breathes heavily through her open mouth. "Oh God, nothing. Mischa..."

"Okay, take it easy. Remember, it's what we expected for that eye. Now, let's take a look at the left one. Ready?"

The last chance. "Ready," she says.

She feels the pad leave her eye, the eyelid is light, unburdened

but for an instant she keeps it closed, she buys herself another instant of ignorance. She can hear the people in the room whispering, there is the scent of flowers. She has Mischa's hands.

Into thy hands o Lord I commend my spirit. . . .

"Okay, Bettina. Open the eye. Open it. That's right. Now, tell me what you see. Anything at all."

She experiences a strange sensation in her eyeball as she raises the lid, there is a fuzziness as if something has been leaning on her eye. She blinks the eye several times to clear away the blur before realizing what that means.

She sees, she *sees*

increasingly pure light comes into her body again through her wide-open eye

blurring faces shift around her

an overhead light in an ugly old fixture

a window glass backed in black night, reflecting moving people

the night stand with a flower on it

a pink flower in a glass

a rose

the wavery image resolves and she blinks, watching the petals emerge from the mass, each sharp-cut, scissor-clean.

"Oh, God," she whispers. "How beautiful a flower is...."

"She can see!" cries someone, a woman, voice delighted.

Bettina looks at her. She's a nurse. Miss DiMarco? Bettina turns her head slowly, looking at all the people who have gathered in her room. She had not guessed there were so many here with her, waiting for the outcome of her operation. She had not known it would matter to so many.

"Bettina, can you see me?" It is Dr. Adams bending his face over her, a thin, youngish man, an ugly man, the most beautiful man in the world.

She touches his shabby green hospital gown. "You need a shave, doc," she whispers.

"Those are the nicest words I've heard in a long time," he tells her, and slaps her lightly on the arm.

She continues to look around her, absorbing the wonderful half-forgotten details of living faces, pores, nostrils, eyelashes, creases in lips. The fat old doctor is Dr. Greshak. "You know you've been absolutely the worst patient I've ever had," he tells her.

"You're something of an old bastard yourself, you know." She loves him. Some day she'll tell him that, the old bastard who wouldn't let her die.

People are coming and going in the room, laughing, calling down the hall. Somewhere on the floor someone is clapping his hands as if in applause.

She sees Greg. "Okay, so the good guys won this one," he says. "It doesn't convince me of a thing, you know." He can't maintain it. He embraces her, really a surprise, considering. She clutches him weakly, kissing his cheek. Almost immediately he regains control and draws away from her. "I may throw up," he says.

In the excitement she has lost hold of Mischa's hands. She turns, looking for him. "Mischa?"

The other people who have been hovering over her draw away from the bed, murmuring, she hears the voices, the chorus of conspiracy. And suddenly she sees Mischa, she *sees* him.

He is a thin young man in a limp orderly uniform. He has his gaze down and is crying, she can see the line of tears escaping from under his glasses and running into his beard.

"Mischa..."

The face is that of a stranger. She has touched it and imagined it but does not recognize it. The shape of the body, however, is familiar to her, as he embraces her, she hangs on to him with all the strength in her weak arms. "God, Mischa, we made it," she whispers, and he whispers back, "Yes . . . yes . . ."

"Careful, kids," Dr. Greshak warns from somewhere in the background. He has a shot of morphine for her. The excitement made her forget the pain briefly, but suddenly it will not be denied, it roars through her head like holocaust, she is ready for relief, she is wild for it

but remembers to ask as the needle goes into her arm, "Please, could Mischa stay. . . ." and her eyelids close on the beatific vision of light and she slides into sleep still holding on to the young man kneeling beside her bed.

There is a small mirror over the sink near the door of her room. She lies in her bed, watching that mirror. It glows in the morning, reflecting the warm sunlight coming through the window opposite. Flowers flash into double-life as nurses carry them past it. Visitors stop for a moment to touch their hair, glance without thought at themselves as they pass. In the evening it slowly becomes blank, opening a hole in the wall.

Tonight after the visitors have gone, and before back rubs and the medication cart, after the woman in the next bed who is irritable with hemorrhoids repaired has fallen grumbling to sleep, Bettina gets up and goes to look at herself in the glass. Dr. Greshak has had her up in the chair during the day, but that was with the help of the nurse. This one she does alone, staggering, demi-fainting, grabbing hold of the bed as she moves across the floor. It is a dumb thing to be doing, anybody would bring her a mirror during the day if she asked for one. What if she falls, what if

but she has an appointment with this particular 12 × 24 inches, a private confrontation

and finally she stands before it.

For the first instant, gasping, trembling, the face in the mirror is not a face, is disconnected from her, she does not quite know what it is. And then she recognizes herself.

God!

The top of her head is disguised with bandage. The bald shaved skull, the dreadful wound where they have picked at her brain, is covered with strips of white cloth, but they cannot bury the cut deeply enough, it is still there, she feels the plummeting pain, a pain as infinite as interspace, waiting for the oblivion of night medication.

Beneath the neat headdress is her face, her face that she has not seen in a year, she has almost forgotten it, like the face of her father, buried under the earth for twelve years, her pale and thin face, her sick face, the pain throbs out of the eyes, the dead one and the live one. She stands there, panting, in front of the glass, looking at this face, a ghost of a face, unsubstantial as ectoplasm

and finally she half-crawls back to her bed and pulls the covers over her head.

Bettina looks up to see Hoss standing in the doorway, watching her. How long her old roommate has been there, she has no idea. Hoss is hesitating. "Should I throw in my hat first?" she asks. Her voice is hearty, but there's a hole in it, the bravura could collapse inwards at a word.

"Oh, for God's sake, come on in, Hoss."

At first they are uncomfortable together, making gesture-talk, health and wealth and weather. Then they glance sideways at each other and laugh. Immediately, they can embrace, pick up the pieces, care again. "Lord, I was afraid I'd had it with you, Bettina. Not that I'm ashamed, you understand. I mean, about

Greg and me. It was the right thing at the time. But it's over, now." Hoss looks sheepishly at Bettina and begins to smile, fluttering her eyebrows, flicking the ash off an imaginary cigar. "Or almost..."

"Good Lord, Hoss, live your own life. I'm not in the position to make judgments."

"It wasn't your judgment I was experiencing. It was guilt. I mean, we really deserted you, there. You know modern society, instant gratification...."

Guilt. The word echoes. "Forget it," says Bettina, and deliberately turns attention to the long cardboard tube Hoss has been shifting self-consciously under her arm. "Hey, what'd you bring me, a thin machinegun?"

"That was my second choice. Look, I figured you'd have all the flowers and candy you could want from the men in your life. I brought you something you really need."

She takes a rolled-up poster out of the tube and lets it unroll in front of Bettina, a huge photograph of a crowd looking upwards at the camera, hundreds of faces, young, old, tousled, prim, but with a wonderful sameness to all of them, they look out in delight, almost in ecstasy, one of life's super-moments.

"It's beautiful. But what are they looking at?"

Hoss examines the back of the poster, looks

at the cardboard tube. "It's called "People." The photographer's name is Ethan Maguire. The company that printed it is Gopher Enterprises, Inc. New York City. And that's it. Maybe that's part of the value of the thing, to keep you busy, guessing."

"It can't be a rock concert, there are too many old faces."

"Maybe it's a free happening in the park. Shakespeare. Or the ballet." Hoss looks again and retracts, pointing to a plump middle-aged man in a large-checked open-necked shirt on one side of the picture: "No, not ballet. I can't imagine middle America that delighted with ballet. Or Shakespeare, either."

A religious revival? Waiting for someone to jump from a high building? The winning number in a lottery? Hoss leaves the poster taped to the wall beyond the foot of Bettina's bed. The faces seem to shift and change as the hours pass and the quality of light in the room varies. The nurses and Mischa and passing visitors all have comments about the poster, but essentially the experience is between Bettina and the faces, she watches them and they watch her

and they are whatever she wants and needs them to be.

*   *   *

She is sitting up in bed, silently holding Mischa's hand, when the phone on the night table rings. She picks it up with her free hand and says, "Hello?" expecting Hoss or Greg. Without preamble, clearly as if he is calling from the lobby downstairs, Piero says, "Bettina?"

"Piero? Where are you?"

and even as she asks him, she realizes the spasmodic movement of reaction the hands have made together, and does not know whether it was her hand that moved or Mischa's

or both.

"I'm in Florence. You mother called to tell me the good news."

She has the unreal experience of operating on two levels. One level feels Mischa drawing away from her and she grabs more securely onto his hand, keeping him. The other level knows Piero.

"Yes. I can see again. Only in one eye, the left one. But who cares. I can see."

"You cannot know how happy that makes me."

Mischa has his face turned away from her. She has hold of his hand, but he will not let her see his face.

There is silence on the line. He is waiting for

her to speak. "Uh . . . I want to thank you, Piero."

"Thank me? But what for?"

"For coming when I was hurt. For . . . the flowers . . ." *See, Mischa. Nothing important. I'm just being polite.*

"I wished to do so much more, but I was so helpless. And you were so . . . separate. . . ." His voice sounds somewhat more accented than she remembers it, a quality of the carbon granules vibrating in the receiver, undoubtedly, exaggerating his pronunciation of English. But it is Piero. God, is it ever Piero.

They are not at ease with each other, they have a hard time maintaining conversation. "How are your parents?"

"My parents? Oh, they are well. Very well."

"And . . . Florence?"

"Beautiful. The river is full of light. It looks like honey."

For one flashing instant she sees him. He has taken the extension out onto the balcony and is standing looking at the Arno as he talks.

"Look, Bettina. I don't know if you heard, but my family has a place in the mountains, very beautiful, you can see for fifty miles in three directions. As soon as you are stronger, why don't you have Greg put you on a plane, and I'll meet you in Milan and take you there."

"Aren't you going to Munich for a year?"

"I will send my mother's cook, Gelsemina, to take care of you. You remember Gelsemina, don't you? The fat girl with the round face?"

"Of course I remember Gelsemina, she's the one who thought it was unladylike of me to run with you."

"Yes, that's right, she's that one. She can take care of you while I'm away. By the Christmas holiday, you should be well enough for me to take you to the sun. To North Africa, perhaps, to Morocco...."

She sees Mischa's hand go up to his eyes. The other hand in hers is absolutely still, it's dead. God, she's implied something, she hasn't been careful enough.

"No, Piero. Things are different now. So much has happened. My life is completely changed."

He is silent for a moment. How much does he know? "Ah, Bettina," he says at last. "That accident of yours was a catastrophe, *una maledizione*, but we must not let it put a wall between us. You did not want me at first, and I have understood that. But now you can see again, you can walk. We will go on, forget everything...."

"I can't forget everything. God, I'll never be exactly what I was before."

"You expect permanent injury?"

"No, no, that's not what I mean. It's just that things cannot go back to what they were."

"So, we begin again." She recognizes the sound of that, his assured optimism, it washes over her, inundates her, she is carried along, struggling desperately, trying to get back to firm shore . . . and a strange flush of heat leaps into her face, her neck, her back, she is drowning, she is fainting. . . .

"Oh, God, I feel sick. . . ."

"*Carissima?* Are you all right? *O dio*, I do not mean to upset you."

"I'll write to you, Piero. As soon as I feel better I'll write and explain everything."

He understands what's happening and he fights, she can feel the intensity of his response: "What are you saying to me, Bettina? Are you ending it between us? You cannot do that. We must talk, you and I. Look, I'm coming to America. I'll be there on Thursday, and we'll talk."

"Please, Piero, don't come. It won't make any difference. I'll write you a letter and explain it all. Don't come. Let me write."

"For the love of God, Bettina, don't hang up on me. Please. Talk to me. . . ."

"Good-bye, Piero. Good-bye." And she puts the receiver carefully into its cradle.

For a few moments she lies very still, looking up at the hospital ceiling, balancing the tears within the skin around her eyes so that they won't spill over and show. She can hear Dr. Greshak's stentorian voice: "Jesus Christ! What are you trying to do, give me a heart attack?" somewhere down the hall. Oh God, after all the nightmares, after all the worry, it is over with Piero, and how simple it was, simple as death.

"Well, that's the end of that," she says, making it sound like nothing. "I'll write him that I release him, he's free for somebody else. That shouldn't be a hardship, there's got to be dozens of Italian girls waiting in line...."

and Mischa says, "Lucky man."

She is waiting for him to go on, say something else, continue their lives, but he sits there unmoving, absolutely quiet, so quiet that it has to be stopped.

"Please, Mischa. Say something. You know this is hard on me."

"Yes, I know."

"Then what's wrong?"

"Why is something wrong?"

"Stop playing games with me. I know you're angry. Why?"

And finally he says, "Why did you not tell him about us?"

He is stabbing her in her hurting heart. "Oh, for God's sake. I couldn't do that, not on the phone. He's Italian. I'd have just been torturing him, saying it out loud. What is it, do you want me to torture him? You've won, why do you need his blood?"

Immediately she is penitent, embracing him, begging him, "Oh, Mischa, I'm sorry, I didn't mean to say something like that. It's just been kind of rough, I can't handle more. Look, I'll write him everything in the letter. Everything. I'll write him a real dear John letter...."

and realizes he does not know what that means, she puts her head wearily on his shoulder, saying, "Mischa, how are you ever going to write the great American novel if you don't even know what a dear John letter is," and slowly his arms come up and hold her.

Afterwards she doesn't quite remember what woke her. Did he touch her? call? or was she just responding, spirit to spirit, to him standing beside her bed? It doesn't matter what causes it, slowly she is coming awake, swimming upwards through the heavy waves of sleep.

"Mischa? Is that you?"

"Yes. Yes. Do not be afraid."

"I'm not afraid. I'm doped out, that's what I

am. God. I don't know what Dr. Greshak is giving me, but I feel as if I could be blown up and never feel a thing."

"He wants you to rest."

She has to struggle to hold on to wakefulness. "It must be 2 AM. How did you get in here?"

"Don't ask me that."

That's right. He knows this place better than anybody, its steam tunnels, its closets, its alleyways. "The Phantom of St. Mary's, eh?"

"I beg your pardon?"

It's too complicated to explain. It's too late or too early, whichever. "Come back later," she tells him sleepily. "I'll talk to you later."

"I must talk to you now, Bettina."

"Oh, Mischa, this is cruel. Can't you wait?"

"No. Wake up, Bettina. Now."

The woman in the next bed murmurs in complaint, and Bettina is aware of her, but more than that, she has caught something in Mischa's voice and pulls herself up in bed.

The room is completely dark, so black she almost forgets that she can see again. After a moment she remembers, and fumbles for her bed lamp. "No, please," he says, but she has the light on before she quite understands him.

He is standing alongside her bed. The bulb of her bed lamp is reflected in both of the lenses of his Harold Lloyd glasses, like a projection of the antennae of an extraterrestrial being. But it isn't his eyes that terrify her. It's the guitar he's wearing slung on his back.

With a strange piercing clarity, she knows what's happening. She knows it and she fights it, but through the incredible weight of her drugged body, almost as if she's living in slow motion.

"God, Mischa. What do you think you're doing?"

He pushes his hair back, his hand remaining clutching his forehead. "I'm going away. To California. Is time now."

The woman in the next bed turns over violently, jerking her blankets up around her ears. "Do you mind?" she says.

Mischa carries a chair over close to the bed and sits. Bettina pulls herself upright with effort and hangs her legs over the side of the bed, embracing him, putting her cheek next to his familiar beard. Her arms are unbearably heavy. She is leaning on him, fighting for control of herself, feeling he is slipping away from her.

"Oh God, Mischa. This isn't fair. I can't think straight."

"Is why I come now. . . ."

"But why are you going? Why?"

And he repeats it. "Is time, now."

She tries to argue with him without arousing the bitch in the next bed, she whispers in his ear, "Talk to me, talk to me...."

and he tells her

Dr. Greshak has gotten him a job in a marina of some friends of his in San Francisco. Misha has spoken to the man on the phone, and he seems businesslike but fair. The work will be hard, but the pay is sufficient, and there are days off, evenings, he will be able to work on his novel of the human soul.

One of the other orderlies has sold him an old navy duffel bag. She sees the end of it protruding around the corner of her bed. It looks limp, as though there isn't much in it. As soon as he's finished here, he's going to go out on the highway with his bag and start thumbing west. With luck he ought to be in San Francisco before the end of the week.

It's happening too fast. She's too weak, too drugged. She can't think of the right questions to ask him, she's lost in unimportant details, what about the gatehouse, what about the furniture he's collected

and he caresses her back gently, telling her, the O'Rourkes will have to get themselves another gardener, he's notified the agency that hired him, and as for the furniture, well, Good

Will has already come and reclaimed it, delighted to get double sales out of the same things.

And finally, desperately, she asks him the real question: What about her? What will she do with the rest of her life?

He is very calm, answering her, incredibly sensible. He's talked to Hoss about taking her in when she's released from St. Mary's on friday. Hoss and three other students are renting an apartment from Columbia University, and there's a hassock in the living room that can be opened up into a bed. It's a very everyday occurrence, having somebody using the apartment hassock, she's welcome to stay as long as she wants. It's a better place for her to go than to Greg's rooms at Miss Moss's, considering; with the disparate hours of the classes of the girls, there's almost always somebody in the apartment, she won't be alone very often.

It's all so neat, so logical. She feels as if a door is closing between them. "Oh, Mischa, couldn't you have waited to go to California? Couldn't we have gone on the way we were, for a little while longer?"

No. No. He is doing it this way on purpose. You see, if she goes back to the gatehouse with him, she will never leave him, and he can never know whether it is because she really wants to stay, or has some sense of owing, some sense of not wanting to hurt him. They came into each other's lives when both of them needed somebody, desperately. Now all debts are paid. Nobody owes anybody anything.

She kisses him frantically, on the ear, on the beard, on the forehead. "But I love you, Mischa. I love you."

"And I love you. . . ."

It seems to her that he's crying, but he is so quiet she isn't sure. "You're doing this because of Piero, aren't you? But why? I told him things had changed, you heard me."

"Oh, Bettina, you say that because I am listening. Perhaps you say it anyway, even if I do not listen, but I do not know that, for sure. You do not know that. You always think of him, always, in all the time you are with me."

"God, Mischa, that has been a need, too, something far away from all the hell. . . ."

and he answers her steadily, he understands that, it is the dream in the head of the sleeping princess. But the princess is awake, now.

He reaches into his shirt pocket and takes out a slip of paper which he puts on her night table. There's the address of the marina in San Francisco written on it. If she wants him, she can reach him there. But it must be a decision, she must not drift into it. "And do not write Piero Ferrari the dear John letter, not yet. Do not cut lines to shore until you know for sure where you wish to sail."

And she whispers, "You're being Russian again...." but she can no longer fight the medication, she is overwhelmed. She leans against him, almost into unconsciousness, feeling her hands falling away from him, she's back into sleep, into dreams of the sea....

He lays her down in her bed again, gently lifting her legs onto the mattress and covering her with the sheet. Then he kisses her, first on the blind eye, then on the good one, closing out her vision of him. She opens her good eye again, when, in a moment, in an hour? She does not know. The room is dark. The light is out. There is no sound at all but the restless woman in the next bed, blowing her nose.

When Bettina wakes again, it is daylight. She has an uneasy sense of something not remembered. Then she sees the slip of paper on the night table.

Greg carries her almost the complete way up the stairs to Hoss's apartment. It is on the fifth floor without an elevator, and after climbing the first flight, Bettina is too exhausted to go any further. She hangs on to her brother, apologizing, as he puffs his way upwards, and sits on his lap when he has to collapse on the step and rest.

"God, I don't believe I'm doing this," he keeps saying. "God . . ."

The staircase has been newly repainted, but is obviously old. Through the window at the turn in the stairs they can see a dark inner court. It is a neat, ugly, old New York City apartment house.

The girls from 5E are at the top of the stairwell, calling down to them. When Greg finally comes around the last bend, gasping and staggering, they run down and take Bettina out of his arms, Hoss doing the actual carrying, with a fluttering assist from the other two girls.

The fourth girl in the apartment has moved out suddenly, down to a SoHo loft where her boyfriend lives, so her room is now vacant. Bettina can stay there until they find somebody else to rent it. Hoss carries Bettina into the room and puts her down on a mattress on the floor. The other girl has taken her bed along with her, and the mattress is all Hoss could hustle up in a hurry. It's an old and lumpy mattress, under the thin bedspread, but Bettina is so tired from her ride into the city from St. Mary's that it doesn't matter, she lies trembling under the comforter they've put on top of her, and there's a whistling in her ears.

Suddenly she comes awake again, without having known she was asleep. There's a churchbell ringing the quarter hour, nearby. She pulls herself up to the window and looks out; on eye level to her window across 114th Street, she can see two of the panels of the church tower, the angel and the eagle. Which symbol is which saint? *Matthew, Mark, Luke and John, bless the bed I lie upon* . . . Mark is the lion. The Venetian Lion of St. Mark . . .

She cannot go any further than that. She slides back into the warmth of the hole where she was under the comforter on the mattress, thinking, as she has almost constantly since he left, about Mischa. Is he in San Francisco, yet? God, but she misses him, it is almost impossible to live, being this alone. . . .

The ceiling of the room where she lies is enormously high above her head, it seems to go tremendously high into space. Twilight is turning down the light outside, and the room is softening about her, obscuring. Everything is painted completely in white, walls, closet, ceiling. The room is infinitesimal in size, the head and two sides of the mattress press against three of the walls, the closet door is barely able to swing open without striking her feet; and

270

yet, she likes it here, this is a remarkably pleasant little hole.

There is movement in the hall of the apartment. One of the girls has acquired an old sofa from someplace, and two young stalwarts have actually dragged it up the five flights of stairs. They pass the open door at the foot of Bettina's bed, carrying the sofa to the living room. Hoss waves into the room as they go down the hall, "Guys, this is Bettina Weston. She's staying with us awhile. Gary and Tom. It is Tom, isn't it?"

"Actually, it's Andy. But you can call me Tom if you want to. Hey, Bettina, what'd you do, stick your head in a snow-blower?"

Somehow, she doesn't feel self-conscious. "Nope. Just lost an argument with a truck."

"Foolish lady. Well, see you. Where do you want this damned thing, Hoss?"

Jeans and beards and the flash of good American teeth. The sofa rises into the air and moves away down the hall.

"Christ, we ought to get a medal for this."

"How about a beer?"

"Actually, I had something more carnal in mind."

"It's a cold beer or a cold shower."

"Now, she tells me."

Bettina gets up slowly and makes her way

down the darkening hall. The first door on the left is the kitchen, where Hoss is opening up beers. It is a bright kitchen, with a pegboard on one wall, neatly hung with dozens of fancy French utensils on hooks. Something smells very good.

"Oh, Bettina. Are you sure you should be up?"

"I'm okay. Say, what smells so good?"

"I don't know, it's Lynne's night to cook." Hoss opens up the oven and peers inside. "I can't tell you, exactly, but it looks like some kind of a casserole. You're in luck. Lynne's really the best cook in the apartment, and you've hit her night."

In the hall outside the living room there's a poster of the Dallas Cowboys cheerleaders, all wearing neatly pencilled-in mustaches above their smiles. Greg has left. The other young people are lying around the living room trying to decide where to put the sofa. One of the boys reclines on it, ankles crossed, while the rest of them shove the sofa back and forth across the floor, getting the effect of the different locations. "Hurry up and make up your minds," says Gary—or is it Andy?—"I'm getting seasick."

"Leave it right there," says Hoss. "It's beautiful there."

"In the middle of the room?"

"We're starting something new. Come on, guys. Here's your beer."

The living room is large, airy, with tall windows on two sides. There are plants everywhere, hanging at the windows, on the bookcase, on the TV. There's a Mostly Mozart poster thumbtacked to the center wall. A cat, black and white, not particularly attractive, is sitting on the coffee table in an Egyptian-tomb pose.

Bettina knows Greta, one of Hoss's roommates, they took Greek Mythology together. The other girl, Lynne, is an art history graduate student. Gary is here because of her. Somewhere in the past they used up sex, and now they are left with a somewhat special friendship. Gary's a law student living up at International House on 120th street. Andy lives on the same floor.

The favor of bringing the sofa up the stairs is repaid with a good dinner, and afterwards the two young men get into a strong discussion on the philosophy of the ghetto. Hoss doesn't want to participate, she has a hockey game coming in on the cable. Lynne sits at the dining room table and makes careful measurements of a xeroxed print of Leonardo's *Last Supper*, establishing the relationship of the proportions of the background. Her shining light-brown hair falls occasionally across the paper as she works and she pushes it aside, not even aware of her movement, completely absorbed by what she is doing. Greta goes to take a shower and comes back in a bedraggled bathrobe, blow-drying her hair, oblivious of the boys still arguing and eating Cheetos.

Bettina goes to bed but cannot sleep. There is more noise everywhere than she has been accustomed to in the last year. Even after the unresolved discussion in the living room has petered out and the participants have departed, calling and shushed up and down the height of the stairwell, there is still the unending sound of traffic on Broadway, the blast of the air brakes of the bus, people walking and laughing together, the siren of a passing police car, the church chimes striking the quarter hour, a hundred noises, unidentified and identified, through the length of the night.

Bettina gets up and goes back down the hall to the living room. There is a level of light that never ceases in the city, streetlights, apartment lights, students working on overnighters, twenty-four-hour businesses, cars, buses. The city glows throughout the night. Airplanes passing overhead see its incredible number of lights twinkling in the darkness. From twenty miles away the country sky of the suburbs is lit up in pale yellow, there is an aura of yellow in the direction of the city.

Some of the light is coming through the tall windows that front on Broadway. Bettina sits in a chair near one of them and looks down at the slowly moving night traffic. She can feel the cool air through the open window, autumn going stale, she smells the exhaust of the passing vehicles, the damp scent of the sea reaching up the Hudson River down at the foot of the street, the slight stench of so many people living together in so small a place. It is a familiar smell, which she had forgotten.

"You okay?"

It's Hoss, yawning, in a shorty nightgown. The realization that Hoss is watching out for her even at night touches Bettina. "I'm okay."

"Can't sleep, huh. How about some white wine?"

They sit together near the window as they drink it, whispering so as not to bother the other girls in their rooms. There is no need to put on a light; the city illuminates them.

"It's so strange, being here, Hoss. Maybe that's why I can't sleep."

"I'm sorry it's such a madhouse. I wish we were more peaceful, I know you've got some heavy thinking to do."

"No, no, it's perfect. I feel as if I've come home. . . ."

Hoss misunderstands her. "Well, kid, it's your home for as long as you want it."

"Thanks, but what I meant was . . ." What did she mean? "I feel like I used to feel, before the accident. When I was at Barnard, I mean. It's really weird, as if the wheel has jumped backwards a cog, and everything has been erased, obliterated, I'm going to live the progression again, but straight through, tomorrow morning I'll get up and walk over to Milbank for bio."

"Except that you've got the problem of your two guys, now. Hell, I should have a problem like that."

But there's something about the night, about the cold wind blowing on them, they are penetrated, made honest. "No," says Hoss after a moment. "No. I just said that because it sounds right, I thought you'd expect me to say it. I don't want the problem, just because it's men after you. God, why is that supposed to be good?"

The bluff husky girl. Man-crazy. Funny. Accepted. Having to prove that she can get a man if she wants one, and maybe that makes Greg a victim as much as she is. She lives a caricature of herself. What then is she really like? Lord. She doesn't know. But it is infinitely more complicated than Hoss.

And Bettina? What is a Bettina? Is it a Mischa, is it a Piero? But they are outside of her, each of them in his own way will take her along with him, a completely different experience for her according to her choice: Florence, California. She will respond with the appropriate part of her soul to the qualities of the man she chooses.

"Dear God . . ." whispers Bettina.

It is beginning to be dawn in the city, soft light shafts down the tunnel of 114th Street.

"Come on," says Hoss. "To bed."

Bettina lets Hoss half-carry her to the little room, put her down on the mattress. "Mary Cartwright, I love you," she says.

"Don't let anybody hear you say that, you know what they'd accuse us of," answers Hoss, covering her up with the comforter. The big girl sits back on her heels for a moment. "And so, complete liberation becomes complete tyranny, right? What the hell. You know I love you too, kid. . . ."

Bettina is looking at her body. She is in the bathtub, the first full examination of her body since the accident. Even after she regained her sight, it has always been nurses with washcloths.

"You okay in there?" Greta asks her through the door. Greta is the only one of the girls left in the apartment. A little while ago Hoss looked in at Bettina's tiny room, on her way to an early class. Lynne is at the library.

"I'm fine, Greta. Don't worry about me."

"I've got my orders from Hoss. She told me to make you a good breakfast."

"I'll be right out."

She decides she has good feet. Funny, she never looked at them before, not to see them. But they're good. *I have good feet.*

And Cathy whispers, "She told me my hands might do, after all . . ."

Bettina puts her feet back under the warm water, feeling the sensation of breaking the surface of the water. The Eskimos think that as long as somebody remembers you, your spirit still lives. *I'll do that for you, Cathy. You are a part of my life, a little fingerprint on my soul. . . .*

The left leg is still thinner than the right leg. Not really freakish, but there, to the knowing eye. The arm, too, is a bad copy of the right arm. And this is now, when so much recovery has already taken place. When the casts came off, she must have looked as if she could tip over sideways, she was so badly balanced . . .

poor Mischa, it must have been like making love to a kindergarten drawing. . . .

She continues her examination of herself, twisting her head to follow the curve of the cut for the double repair of her kidney, around her back. God, but it's ugly. Would it disgust Piero, beautiful Piero, in his mountain retreat? Probably not, she'll grant him that, but she knows how *she* would feel, the escapes into darkness, the subterfuges on her part, that she knows for sure

and stands up in the tub, the wounded warrior, the water runs down her body, her scarred and healing body.

After breakfast, Greta goes to her part-time job, and Bettina is left alone in the apartment. Greta is apologetic, leaving her, but Bettina is delighted for the time by herself in the messy apartment. She wanders around the living room slowly picking up coffee cups and newspapers and bits of lint. It is very quiet. The city is busy beyond the walls, but here there is sunlight on the white walls, a feeling of safety high up in the air, timelessness, the rest of the world ticks on but she is in a safe bubble.

There is a fire escape running along two of the windows, one in the living room, one in the dining room. Bettina leans her palms on the windowsill in the living room, looking out at the plants one of the girls has set out on a corner of the fire escape. Below, through the slats of the fire escape, she can see a Broadway bus easing away from the curb. An old woman drags a shopping cart along the sidewalk. Almost directly across the street a young man in uniform walks unknowing in front of a garage where a generation before his fathers in uniform lined up, Ninety-Day-Wonders who passed through Columbia to be fed into the craw of World War II.

The weakening sunshine of autumn on her bandaged head is warm, a siren song. Bettina climbs through the window and sits cross-legged on the fire escape, watching the traffic moving below, unthinking, alive. The building across Broadway is a Columbia dormitory. The girls have already pointed out the windows of interest. At this time of the day they are blank, all except one located two floors down where she can see a barechested young man struggling with barbells. After a while he comes to his window and waves to her, and she waves back, wondering as she does it what he thinks she is; in her jeans and limp shirt and head in bandages she could be another boy. For now she likes the feeling of that, the sexless gesture between two human beings.

Up the street she can see the ornate green

roofs of Columbia. She is within the outlands of the university, that intense island in the city, where at exam time the air is filled with anxiety and incredible concentration, the feeling creeps out of the clustered buildings into the souls of those who pass. Bettina sits in the sunshine, looking up the street at Columbia

and suddenly, as clearly as if it had called her name, she answers.

She crawls back into the apartment again, her heart beating fast, and puts on a sweater, some shoes. There are scarves in Hoss's messy drawers; she wraps one around her bandaged head, fastens it with a button that says OF COURSE, OF COURSE that she finds on top of the dresser. She puts the housekey from the hook in the kitchen into her pocket, and starts the climb down the stairs.

She has no idea how she will ever make it up these stairs again, on her own. She has no idea even where she will go, what she will do. But she must go. She makes her way, knees shaking, down and down, stopping every once in a while to sit on the steps and gather together some strength again. A beautiful young black woman with a dog comes running up the stairs past her as she sits there, and calls, "Lovely day," as she goes by. Lovely day. Oh yes, lovely day. It has never been so lovely before.

Bettina's heart is thudding with something beyond weakness; she gets up and goes down the stairs, excited as if running to a lover.

On the street beyond the dark foyer a garbage truck is noisily gathering up plastic bags of refuse. Cars double-parked on the other side of the street are blocking the way of a taxi that has come up the hill from Riverside Drive and is honking persistently, *Who the hell do you think you are.* . . .

Bettina pauses at the front door of the apartment house, exhausted, trembling. The street is in shadow, and she is cold. At the corner of the building, up on Broadway, is a bookstore. She makes her way to the sunshine there and leans against one of the wooden counters that have been set up in front of the store with today's bargains, astronomy and accounting self-taught and an old novel that didn't sell. She picks up something, anything, to cover the fact that she is standing there. It is a treatise on the stock market. She opens it and looks down at the sunlit page. The book is rocking in her trembling hands.

She's going to go back to school. She's going to be one hell of a good doctor. She's paying God back whatever she owes, even if He doesn't want it. The decision is made. She feels torn, she bleeds, but she is also filled with relief, with escape, so exultant that she could float away.

She was almost trapped. Almost trapped by the obligation of knowing that someone cared about her greatly, had been fiercely kind to her. She had almost added herself to that long line of good little girls, her mother and her mother's mother and her mother's mother's mother

almost trapped by her bingo heart, by knowing for all of her life that the handsome American captain had indeed come back for his Italian love, not accounting whether after all that had been good or bad, and because of that memory grown into her bones, thinking that it was possible to give up everything she was, to be part of an unrealistic romantic dream.

I want to be
to be
Bettina!

Has she screamed? She looks around her in fright, but the browsers browse, the walkers walk, the day spins on. Beyond the bookstands is the dirty plate glass window of the store. She can see herself reflected in it, a strange thin being in a bright fat turban fastened with a backwards button. Dr. Bettina Weston. Absolutely. Indisputably. Infallibly. Dr. Bettina Weston. She's going to rent the pleasant little hole in apartment 5E from the girls, and study to become Dr. Bettina Weston.

She hears a shuffling beside her. A shabby man of age has sidled up beside her, she can smell his unwashed clothing, she can see him in the glass beside her. He is looking at her. She sees the reflection of his rheumy eyes dribbling tears down the soft bags under his eyeballs. What will the New York City bum do next, mumble a request for a small handout? expose himself? forget her and wander away?

She stands looking at him in the clouded plate glass. "Hello, God," she whispers.

BESTSELLERS FOR TODAY'S WOMAN

THE BUTTERFLY SECRET (394, $2.50)
By Toni Tucci
Eevry woman's fantasy comes to life in Toni Tucci's guide to new life for the mature woman. Learn the secret of love, happiness and excitement, and how to fulfill your own needs while satisfying your mate's.

GOODBYE IS JUST THE BEGINNING (442, $2.50)
By Gail Kimberly
Married for twenty-two years, Abby's life suddenly falls apart when she finds her husband with another woman. Forced into the single's scene, she discovers what life is like as "an unmarried woman."

SARAH'S AWAKENING (536, $2.50)
By Susan V. Billings
From the insecurities of adolescence through the excitement of womanhood, Sarah goes on a wild, wonderful, yet sometimes frightening sexual journey searching for the love and approval of one very special man.

FACADES (500, $2.50)
By Stanley Levine & Bud Knight
The glamourous, glittering world of Seventh Avenue unfolds around famous fashion designer Stephen Rich, who dresses and undresses the most beautiful people in the world.

LONG NIGHT (515, $2.25)
By P. B. Gallagher
An innocent relationship turns into a horrifying nightmare when a beautiful young woman falls victim to a confused man seeking revenge for his father's death.

Available wherever paperbacks are sold, or order direct from the Publisher. Send cover price plus 40¢ per copy for mailing and handling to Zebra Books, 21 East 40th Street, New York, N.Y. 10016. DO NOT SEND CASH!

FICTION FOR TODAY'S WOMAN!

GOODBYE IS JUST THE BEGINNING (442, $2.50)
by Gail Kimberly
After twenty-two years of marriage Abby's life suddenly falls apart when she finds her husband with another woman. From seduction scenes and singles' bars to the problems, successes, and independence of being an "unmarried woman," Abby rediscovers life and her own identity.

WHAT PRICE LOVE by Alice Lent Covert (491, $2.25)
Unhappy and unfulfilled, Shane plunges into a passionate, all-consuming affair. And for the first time in her life she realizes that there's a dividing line between what a woman owes her husband and what she owes herself, and is willing to take the consequences no matter what the cost.

LOVE'S TENDER TEARS by Kate Ostrander (504, $1.95)
A beautiful woman caught between the bonds of innocence and womanhood, loyalty and love, passion and fame, is too proud to fight for the man she loves and risks her lifelong dream of happiness to save her pride.

WITHOUT SIN AMONG YOU (506, $2.50)
by Katherine Stapleton
Vivian Wright, the overnight success, the superstar writer who was turning the country upside down by exposing her most intimate adventures was on top of the world—until she was forced to make a devastating choice: her career or her fiance?

ALWAYS, MY LOVE by Dorothy Fletcher (517, $2.25)
Iris thought there was to be only one love in her lifetime—until she went to Paris with her widowed aunt and met Paul Chandon who quickly became their constant companion. But was Paul really attracted to her, or was he a fortune hunter after her aunt's money?

Available wherever paperbacks are sold, or direct from the Publisher. Send cover price plus 40¢ per copy for mailing and handling to Zebra Books, 21 East 40th Street, New York, N.Y. 10016 DO NOT SEND CASH!

BESTSELLERS FOR TODAY'S WOMAN

ALL THE WAY (571, $2.25)
by Felice Buckvar

After over twenty years of devotion to another man, Phyllis finds herself helplessly in love, once again, with that same tall, handsome high school sweetheart who had loved her . . . ALL THE WAY.

HAPPILY EVER AFTER (595, $2.25)
by Felice Buckvar

Disillusioned with her husband, her children and her life, Dorothy Fine begins to search for her own identity . . . and discovers that it's not too late to love and live again.

SO LITTLE TIME (585, $2.50)
by Sharon M. Combes

Darcey must put her love and courage to the test when she learns that her fiance has only months to live. Destined to become this year's *Love Story*.

RHINELANDER PAVILLION (572, $2.50)
by Barbara Harrison

A powerful novel that captures the real-life drama of a big city hospital and its dedicated staff who become caught up in their own passions and desires.

THE BUTTERFLY SECRET (394, $2.50)
by Toni Tucci

Every woman's fantasy comes to life in Toni Tucci's guide to new life for the mature woman. Learn the secret of love, happiness and excitement, and how to fulfill your own needs while satisfying your mate's.

Available wherever paperbacks are sold, or order direct from the Publisher. Send cover price plus 50¢ per copy for mailing and handling to Zebra Books, 21 East 40th Street, New York, N.Y. 10016. DO NOT SEND CASH!

BESTSELLERS FOR TODAY'S WOMAN

MILEAGE (569, $2.50)
by Toni Tucci
Let Toni Tucci show you how to make the most of the second half of your life in her practical, inspirational guide that reveals how all woman can make their middle years more fulfilling.

ANOTHER LOVE, ANOTHER TIME (486, $2.50)
by Anthony Tuttle
The poignant story of Laura Fletcher, a 47-year-old woman, who rediscovers herself, her life and living, when her husband's arrogance drives her away from him and into the arms of a younger man.

THE AWARD (537, $2.50)
by Harriet Hinsdale
When Hollywood star Jane Benson sees her fame begin to fade, she strives for something to revitalize her image. She buys Vittorio Bellini, the renowned European director, and together they fight to save her career, her life and to help her win . . . THE AWARD.

SEASONS (578, $2.50)
by Ellin Ronee Pollachek
The dynamic, revealing story of Paige Berg, a sophisticated businesswoman, who devotes her life to men, designer clothes and the Salon—one of the most exclusive department stores in the world.

MOMENTS (565, $2.50)
by Berthe Laurence
When Katherine, a newly unmarried woman, finds herself faced with another chance for love, she is forced to make an earth-shattering decision that will change her life . . . again.

Available wherever paperbacks are sold, or direct from the Publisher. Send cover price plus 50¢ per copy for mailing and handling to Zebra Books, 21 East 40th Street, New York, N.Y. 10016. DO NOT SEND CASH!